J
BAK

Baker, Betty.

Seven spells to
farewell

DATE			

SEVEN SPELLS
TO
FAREWELL

BETTY BAKER

SEVEN SPELLS ❧ TO ❧ FAREWELL

MACMILLAN PUBLISHING CO., INC.
New York
COLLIER MACMILLAN PUBLISHERS
London

)BAK

LIBRARY OF CONGRESS CATALOGING IN PUBLICATION DATA
Baker, Betty.
Seven spells to farewell.
Summary: On a long journey to find the kingdom of
Iskany and become a sorceress, a resourceful girl
shares adventures and magic with a talking raven
and a performing pig.
[1. Fantasy. 2. Magic—Fiction] I. Title.
PZ7.B1693Se   [Fic]   81-19305
ISBN 0-02-708150-8   AACR2

To the memory of Grace and Harold Swank,
who owned a Pennsylvania farm with two springhouses
(one with a resident snake) and a gray horse
named Bob and a thousand other marvels that
none of us dreamed would be parts of books

SEVEN SPELLS
TO
FAREWELL

🍂 CHAPTER ONE 🍂

"No!" Dru kept her voice low so the cook behind her at the big iron stove couldn't hear. But her whisper was fierce and determined. "You know what happened when we tried to go to Harvest Fair."

She'd worked a spell to get her uncle to close the inn for a week. A heavy autumn storm had flooded the creek and washed half the stable yard into the ground floor of the inn. The inn had closed, but instead of going to the fair in Kingstown, Dru and her older cousin Sally had spent the week scraping mud from the wood floors.

Sally glanced over Dru's shoulder at Mrs. Grainger, leaned over the table and whispered, "The spell did work, Dru."

"But the *way* it worked was wrong." It was the same with any spell Dru worked. Old Munk claimed she had a natural talent but that didn't seem to be enough to make a sorcerer. "I'm missing something or we wouldn't have spent a whole week scrubbing floors."

Sally took the sugar urn Dru passed her and set it on her tray, rattling the crockery to sound busy. "You just didn't work the right spell. You need one for going to fairs."

"There isn't any." Not in the book old Munk had given Dru when she left Kingstown last summer. And if there had been, it would have worked wrong, too.

"There must be a spell for going somewhere," Sally insisted. "Anywhere!"

Dru shook her head, filled a sugar urn, slid it across the table to her cousin and checked the level in another. If there was a spell for going anywhere, she'd have used it to get to Iskany, to Farewell, the town where Munk's son had a sorcerers' shop near a spell school. Then, when she'd learned to work spells properly, she'd be famous and people would follow her wherever she went and she'd only go where she wanted. She stood, sugar scoop forgotten in her hand, caught up in her dream.

"We've got to do something," Sally wailed aloud.

Mrs. Grainger banged her spoon on the rim of a pot. Dru jumped and spilled the sugar. Sally started grabbing sugar urns, even those Dru hadn't checked yet, and crammed them onto her tray.

"You got to stop lollygagging and get those tables set, that's what you've got to do," said the cook. "That boat horn's going to blow any minute now."

Sally slid the loaded tray off the table and backed through the swinging doors.

"We need butter," Dru told the cook.

"Trust you to wait for the rush to get it." Mrs. Grainger shifted the wooden spoon to her left hand and fished in her apron pocket with the other. She gave Dru the key and a stern look. "And no lollygagging. You hear me?"

"Yes, ma'am."

Dru knew she was watched from the window but she walked as slowly as she dared, lifting her skirts with exaggerated care and taking such wide detours around the few old horse droppings that she expected to hear Mrs. Grainger shout. She did, but the cook's voice was muffled and asking Sally to watch what she was doing.

Dru smiled and headed for the creek. Sally always found some way to distract the cook so Dru could steal a few extra minutes outdoors.

"Help! Hurry!"

It came from around the stable where Willie kept a bench to loaf on overlooking the creek and the woods beyond. But it couldn't be the stable boy calling. The carriage was gone, waiting for the boat, and the stable boy's voice wasn't old and harsh.

"Tromp it!" the voice called again.

Dru moved quietly to the stable and peeked around the corner. A pig had trapped a mottled brown snake in the corner made by the end of Willie's bench and the stable wall. The end of the snake's tail shook furiously but the only sound was the hiss from its open mouth. Dru grinned.

The pig leaned forward, snuffling. The snake stopped imitating a rattling snake, flattened its thick neck and swayed like a serpent from the Hot Lands.

"Is it good to eat?" squawked the voice.

3

The pig took two steps forward.

"You leave that snake alone!" Dru stepped around the corner and nudged the pig aside. The snake flopped over, belly up, and lay still. "Poor thing."

"Poor snake!" The harsh voice belonged to a raven standing behind the pig. "What about us? That poor snake tried to kill us."

"It did not! It couldn't. It's just a harmless hognose. . . . Begging your pardon," she added to the pig and immediately felt foolish. She knew crows and ravens could be taught to talk but she'd never heard of a talking pig, not even in Iskany.

The pig grunted, though, as if it understood.

"The snake was just trying to make you go away." Dru looked from pig to bird. "How did you get here? Who do you . . . ."

A horn sounded downriver. Dru picked up the snake.

"Wait!" squawked the raven. "As long as it's already dead . . . ."

"It isn't," Dru told him, though it hung from her hand as if it were.

Drucilla! That was Mrs. Grainger.

Dru ran for the creek, keeping the stable between her and the back of the inn. A path led down the bank and a fainter one along the creek to the springhouse. Dru ran crouched so the bank hid her from the kitchen. The pig and raven watched from the top of the bank, probably to see where she left the snake.

4

She called back softly, "If anyone else finds you here, you'll be tomorrow's dinner. Both of you." Her uncle wouldn't waste the raven.

"Drucilla! Where's that butter?"

She was close enough to the springhouse to answer. *"I'm getting it!"*

She laid the snake near the overflow pipe, right side up. As soon as she removed her hand, it flopped belly up and lay as still as before.

"Silly," Dru told it and went to unlock the springhouse door.

As she pulled open the padlock, she glanced back. The pig and raven were heading for the road, around the far corner of the stable. She wondered why the bird didn't fly. Or at least ride on the pig's back.

The springhouse was chill and dank and smelled of milk. The spring bubbled up in a stone-lined trough that took up half the small building. Bottles, crocks and milk cans stood in the cold water, their rims above the surface. Cheeses hung from the ceiling or rested on the waist-high rim of the trough. Dru found a crock of butter, cast a wistful eye at the cheeses and locked the door behind her.

The snake had left. So had the raven and pig.

"DRUCILLA!"

"Coming!" She hurried up the stone steps set in the bank. Mrs. Grainger stood in the kitchen door, hands on hips, and watched her cross the yard. She held out a hand for the key.

"Never pays to hire relatives," she muttered. "If your uncle had asked me . . . ."

"He didn't even ask me. Relatives aren't hired, they're told." Especially poor relatives with no place else to go. Dru dropped the key in the outstretched hand. "Sally and I aren't paid anything."

"And it's just what you're worth."

The cook pocketed the key and returned to filling soup tureens. Dru made a face at her back.

She slapped chunks of butter on deep round dishes, covered them with pewter domes and started slicing bread into thick chunks. Her uncle was generous with bread and soup. They were filling and cheaper than the meat that followed.

The taproom and dining room grew noisy with voices, locals who'd come to hear the news and a few people going to Kingstown for Spring Fair. But most were boat passengers headed upriver to Summerfalls, the mountain resort where lords and ladies from all five kingdoms idled away the summers. Not that any lords and ladies came to the inn.

The royal and very rich had their own boats. Sally had taken Dru to the docks last autumn to watch the private boats float past, homeward bound, their lighted decks filled with dancers. Dru had tried to stop one for Sally.

Her book, *101 Spells for Everyday Need*, had no spell for stopping boats or summoning royalty. Dru had worked a combination of Success at Fishing and Safe

Return From a Journey. Willie had arrived at dawn, dripping wet, with three giant dogfish for sale. They'd eaten fish stew for nine days and Willie was still at the inn as stable boy.

Dru refused to try again and Sally was left with only her hope that one of the boats would bring a handsome young man, preferably royal, who would carry her away to wealth and happiness in one of the prosperous kingdoms to the east, beyond the Great River. She wouldn't scorn royalty from Iskany, but the boats carried few travelers from that western kingdom. It was a long journey by water and it was said that sorcerers kept the weather perfect in Iskany.

But the three kingdoms to the east were having an early spring and Summerfalls had opened early, much to the delight of Sally and her father: her father because of the extra business; Sally because, with the sudden spring rush upriver, some of the private boats might not be ready. So she carried soup tureens into the dining room with an eager step.

Dru heard her voice among the diners', trading sympathy or jokes while she eavesdropped and searched for stray royalty. She took so long with the second tureen that Mrs. Grainger grumbled about lollygagging.

"You're not obliged to serve it," the cook told her. "Just set it on the table. And get some bread out there. This is a fresh pot of soup and your pa doesn't want it all eaten tonight."

Sally took two wooden trenchers stacked with bread

7

into the dining room. She was back before the door stopped swinging. Mrs. Grainger turned to stare at her. Dru was even more surprised.

Sally told them, "There's a show tonight on the green," grabbed another pair of trenchers and was gone.

Caravans had stopped in the village before and after Harvest Fair. They'd all had something for sale, from charms and soaps to silhouettes cut to order. And all, except the silhouette cutter, had provided free entertainment. Such caravans were a large part of Kingstown fairs, but until last autumn, Dru hadn't realized they traveled all year from village to town, perhaps from kingdom to kingdom.

Sally returned and filled her tray with butter dishes while chattering loudly about the show. "Dr. Blessing and his mystagogic crow. The crow tells fortunes." She gave Dru a meaningful look. "We could learn about things."

Mrs. Grainger humphed. "What kind of doctor is this Blessing?"

"Trained in Iskany and trusted in all five kingdoms."

"Then what's he doing here?"

As she lifted the tray, Sally mouthed to Dru, "We've got to go!"

Dru agreed, though not for the same reasons.

Mrs. Grainger set a platter of boiled beef on the table and told Dru, "When you finish the bread, you can start on this."

Then she went to sit on a stool in the coolest part of

the kitchen, near the door. It was where she sat to super-vise the cleaning each evening, keeping Sally and Dru scrubbing and polishing for hours. If Mrs. Grainger didn't want to see the show, Sally and Dru weren't going to see it, either.

Dru wiped her face on her sleeve and found the carving knife.

"Bread thick, meat thin," the cook reminded her.

Dru shaved a slice from the meat. She wished she could get to her spell book. Maybe she could adapt a spell she already knew, like the one for spellbound rosemary she and Sally kept under their pillows for pleasant dreams. But she didn't think being sprinkled with rosemary would sweeten Mrs. Grainger.

Sally brought an empty tureen from the dining room. Mrs. Grainger got up to refill it. Dru was still too short to ladle soup from the huge pot and Sally always spilled enough to make Mrs. Grainger decide to do it herself.

"This Dr. Blessing got anything for lumbago?" said the cook.

Sally's and Dru's eyes met, daring to hope. Sally brought more tureens and bread trenchers for refill-ing. On one trip she announced that the passengers wanted the captain to hold the boat until after Dr. Bless-ing's show.

"So it must be worth seeing," she told Dru loudly.

More likely the long trip upriver was dull, but Dru said, just as loudly, "Or he's selling something that works."

Mrs. Grainger went right on arranging a thin layer of meat in the center of each platter and filling the wide margins with mountains of turnips, potatoes and beets.

Dru sighed and lugged the kettle from the stove. She filled two dishpans, one for washing and one for rinsing. She was halfway through the soup bowls and almost in despair when Mrs. Grainger untied her apron, gave instructions about serving the bread pudding and went home to dress for the show.

Sally danced twice around the worktable and dashed off to collect more dirty dishes. Dru washed them at a speed that would have amazed Mrs. Grainger. Sally helped when she could and they ate on the run, grabbing a mouthful when they passed the table. But candles were lit long before Dru threw the dishwater into the yard.

They skipped the cleaning Mrs. Grainger thought necessary and raced upstairs to their attic room. They paused only to splash faces with water, smooth hair with wet hands and grab shawls, then pounded back down the two flights of stairs, out the front door and across the porch. Sally's father yelled something from the taproom but they didn't wait for him to repeat it.

A light blue caravan stood in the center of the green. Torches lit a platform set up at its end. On the platform, a bearded man in a black suit drew bright silk scarves out of the air.

"We're missing it!" wailed Sally.

She galloped across the road, heedless of ruts and

stones. Dru followed more carefully. She'd seen similar magic at Kingstown fairs. The passengers must have seen it before, too. They didn't applaud or crowd up to the platform with the local people. If the man had more magic, he didn't work it.

"And now," he bellowed, "for the wonder you've been waiting for!"

Dru stood on tiptoe to look for Sally.

"A marvel seldom seen beyond the borders of Iskany!" The bearded man waved to red curtains leading to the caravan. "Humphrey the Great!"

From between the curtains came a pig. If he was the same one Dru had met, he'd become ill very suddenly. He swayed and tottered to the center of the platform. There was a sympathetic murmur from the audience.

Dru stopped craning her neck and moved closer. So did everyone else, but she edged sideways here, ducked an elbow there and finally squeezed up to one end of the platform. She had a side view but only two people stood in front of her and she could see between them.

Tapping once for no and twice for yes, Humphrey answered the man's questions. The pig didn't feel well enough to perform and wanted some Elixir. The man protested that he hadn't much of the precious Elixir and all that he had was meant for humans. But the pig's taps became weaker and his legs sagged and trembled.

"Give him some," somebody yelled.

"Yeah, let's see what it can do," said another.

"He's afraid to let us see," called somebody behind Dru.

"Very well," said the man. "But just this once, Humphrey, and only because these good people insist."

People cheered and applauded as he took a flat bottle from behind the table and poured the brown contents into Humphrey's mouth. The pig licked his lips and stood staring over the audience. His eyes blinked slowly and a few people laughed. His ears and tails seemed to perk and his legs straightened. He hiccuped loudly. Dru laughed along with everyone else.

"Are you ready now, Humphrey?" said the man.

Humphrey tapped twice, firmly. Then he answered questions about people in the audience, turning some of them into jokes. He also tapped numbers, adding and subtracting and then giving the distance to Kingstown. That took so many taps that the pig used both front hooves, turning the count into a catchy beat.

Dru tapped her foot. Somebody began to clap the rhythm. Soon everyone was clapping as Humphrey swayed, sideways and back, turn about and forward, tapping with front hooves and counter-tapping with the rear as he danced a frisky jig. Then he backed through the red curtains and was gone.

People clapped and shouted for Humphrey. Dru followed one familiar voice to Mrs. Grainger. The cook stood in front of the platform. If she turned her head just a little, she'd look straight at Dru. Sally waved frantically from the other side of the crowd. Dru didn't dare signal for fear of attracting Mrs. Grainger's attention. But Sally was watching and would guess she was circling the caravan.

The lettering on the side was worn and chipped. The three lines of large letters read:

DR. BLESSING PRESENTS
THE MYSTAGOGIC CROW
AND THE CALCULATING PIG

Smaller letters added:

TRAINED IN ISKANY—
TRUSTED IN FIVE KINGDOMS

At the front end, a gray horse stood hitched in the caravan's shafts. In the dark, Dru couldn't tell if it slept. A torch stuck in the ground lit battered wooden steps that marked a doorway. The door was tied back.

Everybody's attention was on the platform. From the sound, Humphrey was dancing another jig. Dru crept to the open door.

A frame, wide as the door and higher than Dru's head, had been set in the doorway. The frame was filled with diamond-shaped cubbyholes holding little scrolls of parchment. Not all the diamonds were filled. One or two were almost empty. Dru leaned over the steps, hands on her knees, and peered into the caravan. A yellow eye peered back.

❧ CHAPTER TWO ❧

"Show me a bottle or give me a penny," said a harsh voice.

Dru let her breath out. "It's you!"

The dark shape behind the cubbyholes climbed zigzag to the top of the frame, ruffled his feathers and peered down.

Dru straightened. "You aren't a crow."

"And that isn't Dr. Blessing," said the raven.

The clapping and cheering had stopped and the man could be heard talking about the Elixir. Dru stepped back. The same lettering covered this side of the caravan, interrupted by the open door.

She pointed. "But it says . . . ."

"Lettering is expensive. Can't repaint every time there's a replacement."

"Oh." Dru was disappointed. She'd hoped the raven had been traveling as long as the caravan had. "I don't suppose you know the way to Iskany?"

"Certainly. Take a boat downriver."

"Two boats," Dru corrected. One from the dock to

the Great River and a larger, more expensive boat from there. "I don't have any money."

"No fortune without a penny or a bottle of Elixir." The bird sidestepped down one of the slanting perches that zigzagged from top to bottom behind the honeycomb of diamonds.

The man had stopped talking. People were moving around, some toward Dru.

She said quickly, "There's another way to Iskany, over the mountains."

The bird stopped his shuffling. There was a questioning grunt from inside the caravan.

"The snake lover," said the raven. To Dru, he said, "Nobody goes that way."

"Why not?"

"It's a long and dangerous journey."

"How do you know?"

"Because nobody goes that way."

"Then how . . . ."

"You know anybody who's come from the mountains?"

"Only from Summerfalls."

"There you are." He climbed back on top of the rack and squawked, "Show me your bottle or give me a penny."

"Here." Sally reached past Dru. "Here's a penny for each of us."

Sally managed to hide some of her meager tips from her father, but since she wasn't supposed to have them, she could seldom spend the few pennies she saved. She waved aside Dru's thanks.

"It's an investment in our future," she said. "We have to do *something*."

She followed the raven's progress back and forth down the rack, dancing with excitement when he selected a scroll and carried it back to the top. It was tied with a dark blue string. Sally took it from the bird's beak and gave him the second penny. He dropped it through a slot in a tin box and hung upside down from the second perch to reach the center diamond.

There was a disturbance inside the caravan, with snuffles and angry snorts, then a sad sigh as the raven pulled a scroll from the center diamond. The torch flared and Dru saw Humphrey looking at her through the half-filled diamonds.

Sally nudged her. The raven was leaning down from the top of the rack, the scroll in his beak.

"Thank you," said Dru and took it. "Let's watch a little while, Sally."

A line had formed behind them. Everybody had bottles of Elixir except three girls Sally and Dru never had time to become friends with. They gave the raven their pennies and got scrolls tied with pink, green and pale blue. They crowded around one of the torches, giggling and whispering over their fortunes.

"Come on," said Sally. "Let's open ours in privacy."

Dru followed reluctantly. She hadn't yet found a reason or pattern for the raven's choices, but in the short time she'd watched, nobody else had received a scroll tied with gold.

Sally giggled. "Did you see Mrs. Grainger? She has two bottles. I wonder if she'll get two fortunes."

They made up pairs of fortunes for the cook as they walked across the green. They weren't the only ones headed for the inn. The taproom was going to be unusually busy until the horn announced boarding of the boat. Sally's father would be looking for help, if only to wash tankards and glasses.

"We'll have to sneak in," said Sally.

The kitchen door would be bolted by now and all windows shuttered except those overlooking the green. Dru pointed to a group of five men, passengers from the boat. Sally grabbed her hand and pulled her into a stumbling run, clutching scroll and shawl with the same hand. With the torches behind them, they moved into their own shadows until they were across the road. But they caught up to the men and tagged along, keeping the group between them and the taproom door. Sally bent her knees a little and the passengers gave them cover almost to the foot of the stairs. Their conversation was interesting, too.

They were trying to decide if Humphrey had been trained like a dog or spellbound by a sorcerer in Iskany. That led to an argument about whether or not pigs could be trained. Dru was almost sorry to leave them.

They raced up the stairs and down the hall to the door to the attic stairs. Sally latched it behind them.

They climbed the second flight leaning against the walls, laughing and shushing each other.

They placed the scrolls on the bed while they washed in the cracked bowl, brushed their hair and put on nightgowns. Then, careful to make no noise, they moved Sally's clothes chest away from the wall.

It sat in an awkward corner to hide holes left when the flooring had run out. One wide plank stopped a few inches from the wall, the one next to it left a hole three times as large. Sally reached in and drew out a tin box. It held her money and her mother's brooch, Dru's spell book and the candle stubs they stole from downstairs. They were allowed only one candle a week for their room.

While Sally stuck the stubs into dusty bottles, Dru punched the bolsters into back rests and turned to sit against one. Sally divided the bottle candlesticks between the table and the shelf that flanked the bed. Then she climbed in beside Dru and they pulled the frayed quilt to their waists. Solemnly they took up the little scrolls and looked at each other.

"Who first?" said Sally.

"Both together," said Dru. She waited until Sally took hold of a string end, then counted to three and said, "Now!"

She tugged open the gold bow and unrolled the stiff parchment. The brown script was so beautiful it was a moment before Dru knew what it said: "Befriend a dark stranger and reap rewards."

Sally shrieked and bounced to her knees. "I'm going, Dru! I'm going!"

"Shh!" Dru glanced at the stairs. "Where?"

"To meet my husband! Listen." She sat on her heels and read, " 'A journey leads to heart's desire.' Oh, Dru, isn't it marvelous? I wonder where I'm going and what he'll look like. Is there a spell for . . . oh, I'm sorry, Dru. What's yours?"

Dru let her read it for herself.

Sally looked up, eyes wide. "You're going to be rich!"

"It doesn't say that."

"But that's what it means."

It meant there wasn't anything mystic about the raven. Dru remembered playing future teller with friends years ago. The futures they told each other always included a long journey and a dark stranger.

Dru climbed over Sally to the front window. She had to cup her hands around her eyes to see through the glass. The torches had burned out but the green was bright with moonlight. As she'd expected, the caravan was gone. Elixir users would find no one to complain to in the morning.

"Fly by night," Dru muttered. But they wouldn't escape so easily from Kingstown.

Sally leaned over her back to look. "What is it?"

"I'm just checking the moon," Dru lied, not wanting to spoil Sally's joy. She couldn't be certain the fortunes were false. But a spell might be a way to check.

She got the spell book from the tin box, sat down cross-legged and carefully opened the blue paper cover.

"Yes!" said Sally. "Find one so I can see him. If I don't like him, I won't make the journey." She giggled nervously.

She arranged the bottle candleholders around Dru and settled beside her on the bare floor. She tucked her nightgown under her feet and clasped her arms around her bent knees, watching silently as Dru turned the pages.

"Here's one." Dru ran her finger under the crooked lines of type. "You must wait through the dark of the moon . . . ."

"Alone?"

". . . on a rock surrounded by water but never covered by it"—she skipped the incantations—"and your true love shall appear."

"We can't use it." Sally sounded relieved. "All the rocks in the river here have been covered by floods."

"We could roll one down the bank."

"What about splashes? Isn't there another one?"

There was, but Dru liked it even less than Sally did the first one. Two people were needed to work it and Dru wasn't looking for a true love. Sally thought it was perfect. She found an answer to every objection. Dru didn't remember agreeing but suddenly Sally was snuffing the candles between wet fingers and saying, "We have to get some sleep so we can sneak you outside before Mrs. Grainger gets here, to get that stuff for the spell."

"Gentian root."

"Gathered at dawn." Sally made it sound romantic.

They overslept and Mrs. Grainger didn't let them forget it. Lay-abed lollygaggers, she called them and hinted at changes in the kitchen help.

Sally grinned over the porridge bowls at Dru and whispered, "If she only knew!"

With the late start and the cleaning left from the night before, Sally was setting tables for the noon meal before Dru dumped the breakfast dishwater. Dru lingered outside the door, face lifted to the westerly breeze, until Mrs. Grainger called her inside. She didn't expect to get outside again that day, but after the noon meal was cleared, Mrs. Grainger sent her for cheese.

"But it's the wrong time to get that spell stuff, isn't it?" whispered Sally.

"No," Dru told her. "It's just not as good as dawn."

Sally stopped looking anxious and began slicing onions with a flourish.

Dru went straight to the springhouse. The hognose snake was sunning on the bottom step. Dru slid down the bank rather than disturb it. She found the right cheese, locked the door and circled the woodpile. She remembered gentians blooming there in the autumn. It was much too early for the blue flowers but she needed only the roots.

She broke a twig from the nearest bush. She needed no spell book for this. She'd helped her mother harvest plants, both wild and those grown in the garden behind their cottage. Holding the twig in her left hand, she drew a circle around gentian plants, chanting, "*Mystic plant be kind to me; work the spell I ask of thee.*"

The stems were barely long enough to grasp, but Dru tugged the plants free, tapped the roots on a log to get rid of the dirt and tucked them under her apron.

A bird swooped by carrying a bit of twine to its nest. Dru sat on a log and remembered tying bunches of herbs with the same kind of twine and then taking the dried bunches to Munk's shop.

The sign said Sorcerer's Shop but Zuus was too poor a kingdom to attract Iskany's sorcerers. And few people in Zuus could work spells, an ability common in Iskany.

Old Munk could. He bound mints and mullein and goldenrod into healing teas and poultices that he sold for eggs or an onion or one wrinkled potato. But he paid in coin for herbs. Buying them for his son's shop in Iskany was, Dru finally guessed, the real reason for the shop.

Though her mother had had a gift for growing herbs, she'd never been curious about how or why the plants were used. But Dru had pestered the old man with questions. He'd teased her about having an ancestor from Iskany but he'd answered her questions, and last summer, when her mother was ill, he'd taught her to bind rosemary in a Pleasant Dream Spell. Dru had hoped to stay with him after her mother died, but the town council had declared her a ward of her uncle, who was no more blood kin than old Munk. Dru's mother and Sally's had been sisters.

When she had to leave Kingstown, Munk had given Dru the spell book. But there was no spell in it that would take her back to last spring, when she had searched the fields and woods for herbs, her mother beside her.

"DRUCILLA! WHERE ARE YOU?"

Dru ignored the first three calls. Then she wiped her tears, brushed an ant from the cheese and trudged back to the kitchen. She was glad she didn't have to work a midnight spell tonight. The roots had to dry first.

Three nights later they sneaked downstairs. Three days weren't enough to dry roots, not even young ones hung in the hottest corner of the attic. When ground in Mrs. Grainger's stone mortar, they produced a stringy paste instead of a powder.

Sally looked a question. Dru shrugged. They didn't dare speak until the spell was worked.

Nor could they chop the roots. Metal was never used with plants meant for spells. Dru managed to work enough of the paste into the four candles they'd softened on the warming shelf of the stove. They prepared the meal with only a few reminding nudges and hand signals. Sally had planned every move while they were waiting for the roots to dry and for a night when the taproom closed early.

They set four places on the worktable. Dru arranged the four gentian candles and lit them while Sally blew out the ones that had lighted their work. They divided the saltless food on four plates and served them to the empty chairs. Then they stood and stared across the table at each other.

Sally looked nervous but not enough to speak and

break the spell. Dru wanted to. She had no desire to eat with the spirit of the man she'd marry. But the spell needed two to work, and if Dru broke it, Sally would just insist they repeat it another midnight. Dru checked the table, nodded to Sally and pulled back her chair.

Sally clapped both hands over her mouth to hold back a scream. She was staring past Dru, her eyes wide with terror.

❧ CHAPTER THREE ❧

Dru turned. A dark shape filled the window. A head, she thought, because its eyes glinted like metal. Dru stepped closer. They *were* metal: stirrups crossed over the seat of a saddle carried on somebody's shoulders. She couldn't see the real head in the shadows underneath.

"Willie!" Sally dropped onto a chair. "Oh, Dru, I don't want to marry Willie!"

"You won't. You didn't catch all that scream. The spell was broken."

Willie was gone from the window. Dru couldn't see where he'd gone but it wasn't back to the stable.

"Where did he get the saddle?" she wondered.

"He probably stole it from the stable. There were two in there in case anybody wanted to hire a horse to ride." Sally glared at the plate of cold food. "Serves him right."

Dru turned from the window. "Who?"

"My father. They're two of a kind." Her face crumpled. "Oh, Dru!"

Dru circled the table to pat her shoulder and assure

her the spell had been broken. Though Dru wasn't sure herself if Sally had screamed before the spell began working, and if not, what it meant.

They cleared the meal as quietly as they'd prepared it. They pushed all the food onto two plates, salted it and carried it to the attic to eat. When they settled for sleep, they still hadn't figured a way to let Sally's father know Willie had stolen a saddle, maybe two.

"We'll have to check the stable." Sally sat up. "Dru! What if I need one for my journey?"

"You won't. If the fortune is true, it's true no matter what."

"That's right."

Dru didn't have to turn over and look to know Sally was smiling.

Mrs. Grainger knew the kitchen had been used in her absence but couldn't be sure it wasn't Sally's father who'd used it. She banged pot lids and muttered dire warnings about changes. Dru was too tired to care. Twice the cook caught her staring down at the breakfast dishes, half asleep with her hands in the warm water. When Sally took a stack of plates into the dining room and didn't come back, Dru feared she'd gone to sleep at one of the tables. She grabbed a pair of filled spoon holders and went to wake her.

Sally had her ear pressed to the door of the Private Parlor, a room barely large enough to hold two chairs and a small table. She stopped listening to grab Dru and waltz her between the dining room tables.

"I'm going . . . I'm going," she sang softly.

Dru pulled her to a stop. "Where? When?"

Sally twirled away by herself. "To Summerfalls . . . Summerfalls . . . for the season . . . Summerfalls with my aunt . . . ."

Her aunt was her father's sister and very like him. Dru told her, "She just wants a free maid."

Sally giggled. "Not so free. He's making her pay for the cost of replacing me. That's what they're arguing about now."

Dru could breathe again. "Then maybe . . . ."

"There you are, lollygagging, the pair of you." Mrs. Grainger's face scowled at them over the hinged doors. "There's bread needing slicing and those tables won't set themselves."

"Old crow," Sally muttered and started dealing plates onto a long table.

Dru grinned and went back to the kitchen. Her uncle was sure to ask more than his sister would pay. But Dru's relief only lasted through the meal. Sally was helping with the dishes and guessing about the royalty she'd meet, softly so as not to disturb Mrs. Grainger dozing on her stool, when her father called, "Sally? Get in here."

For somebody who wasn't supposed to know, she looked awfully happy. She pulled her face straight, smothered a giggle and banged angrily through the doors. Dru leaned against the dry sink and waited. It seemed ages before Sally's happy face appeared at the hinged doors.

"Come help me pack," she whispered and was gone.

27

Dru washed the pots in record time, left the pans of water in the sink and raced up the stairs to the attic.

Sally had sorted the contents of the chest. One pile was hardly large enough to make a bundle. The rest was heaped on another. She scooped the large pile back in the chest.

"They'll be large for you yet," she told Dru, "so don't let my father know you have them or you'll never get anything new."

Dru didn't think she would anyway. "Don't you need the cloak? It's cooler up at Summerfalls."

"And very elegant. My aunt promised me a *complete* new wardrobe." Sally giggled. "I guess she doesn't want me to disgrace her."

They moved the chest to reach the tin box. Dru took out the spell book and went to a tall leather hatbox in the corner. It was old-fashioned and battered but it had been her mother's. Dru used it now for the herbs she'd collected last autumn.

She found a small linen sack of dried comfrey and crumbled some on a square of linen laid carefully on the wooden floor. She consulted the spell book but not for the Safe Journey spell. She knew that; it was the first she'd ever worked. She was seeking something else, leafing quickly through the pages. She stopped at a spell binding livestock to a farm.

She could adapt it and she had the correct herbs in the hatbox. She took them out and weighed the little sacks in her hand. She didn't want to bind Sally to the inn. She just didn't want her to leave now. Sometime later, Dru could unbind her. Maybe. Dru sighed.

"*Sally!*" Her uncle's voice carried two flights, only slightly muffled. The door at the foot of the attic stairs was ajar.

While Sally shouted an answer, Dru tossed the two sacks back in the hatbox, leaned over the comfrey and chanted softly. Then she drew the corners together, tied the linen into a pouch with a bit of string and presented it to Sally.

"To protect you on your journey."

Sally looked at it doubtfully. "Do I have to wear it?"

"No, you can pack it with your clothes, but then it will protect them more than you, I think."

"That's all right. I'm going to carry them."

"SALLEEEEE!"

"*Coming!*" Sally tucked the pouch into the small bundle and hurried down the stairs.

"That's another thing I'm going to change," she called back to Dru. "From now on I'm Salamantha or Salena. Who ever heard of a duchess named Sally?"

Dru had a hard time keeping up. When she reached the porch, Sally was already in her aunt's carriage. Dru wrapped an arm around a pillar and wondered if Sally would remember to look back. She did. They waved to each other until the carriage turned a corner and was gone. Dru wiped her eyes with the back of her hand and went to throw out the dishwater.

"You're next," Mrs. Grainger said when Dru brought back the empty pan.

"What?" Dru stared at her, confused.

"My fortunes. I got two of them, exactly alike: 'A source of contention is removed.' And you two are the most contention I've ever had. Worse than the lumbago. And if one of those fortunes is true, the other must be."

She sounded so pleased that Dru felt even worse. But the cook wasn't as pleased when Willie appeared wearing a clean shirt and the smell of horses, ready to serve the evening meal.

"Folks don't want to eat in a stable," she muttered. "Spoils their appetites."

"Maybe that's why my uncle did it," Dru said. "After all, he pays one of the captains to blow the boat horn early so nobody gets second helpings or desserts."

Mrs. Grainger humphed, but after a moment's thought told Dru not to slice as much meat as usual. "Until we see how things go."

Dru was glad her uncle hadn't expected her to serve in the dining room. Even if she could manage the heavy trays and tureens, which she doubted, she could never whisk in and out among the tables the way Sally had, laughing and joking with the diners.

Besides, one person couldn't serve and do Dru's work, too, not in summer. With Sally gone, Dru could barely manage. Willie didn't fill bread trays, dry dishes or do any of the little things Sally had done to help. Dru went to the attic later and tireder than she ever had.

She threw herself on the bed, then sat up when her foot hit something. The tin box. They'd forgotten to replace the chest. Dru lifted the box onto her lap. Sally had left half her pennies. Dru blinked back tears, got up and washed and changed into her nightgown.

She lit all the candle stubs, puffed up the bolster and settled against it. The ceremony seemed senseless without Sally to share it but Dru unrolled her fortune and read it aloud.

"Befriend a dark stranger." Thank goodness Willie wasn't dark! But how would she meet a stranger if she wasn't serving in the dining room? She was getting like Sally looking for strayed royalty. But if fortunes came true for Sally and Mrs. Grainger, why not for her?

She tucked the scroll under the bolster, turned on her side and stared at the stained wall. She'd never slept alone before. She sighed. She'd better get used to it, the way people kept leaving her or sending her away.

She hoped she'd fall asleep before the last candle stub burned out.

❧ CHAPTER FOUR ❧

"And then I'll make a belt out of the skin, you see."

Dru glared over the table at Willie. "It's just a harmless hognose."

"It's a snake, isn't it?"

Dru pushed back her chair, dumped her plate and fork into the cold dishwater and told Mrs. Grainger, "We're going to need butter."

"You see? You don't need to wait until we're busy. All you needed was a fine example." The cook beamed at Willie.

But Dru hadn't given up lollygagging. She just wanted to get away from Willie's bragging. She took the key and hurried out.

The hognose was sunning on the bottom step. She could move it behind the springhouse but it would only come back. She jerked open the lock and threw back the door.

It wasn't fair! Creatures who never hurt anyone got killed and chased, while people like her uncle got fat and rich.

She grabbed a butter crock and turned. The crock shattered on the stone floor.

A pig stood in the doorway, blocking the light.

"Didn't mean to scare you," said a harsh voice. The raven ducked under Humphrey and straightened to cock his right eye up at Dru. "Know anyone named Drew? Stable boy, maybe?"

"It's me. Short for Drucilla. What do you want? How did you get here?"

The raven ignored her. "Told you," he said to the pig.

Humphrey snuffled unhappily.

"Beggars can't be choosers," the bird told him. "It's done now."

"What's done?" said Dru. "Why do you want me?"

"We don't," said the raven. "But it seems we're stuck with you."

"For what? Where's the man?"

"He was detained in Kingstown."

"Oh." Dru remembered the spice dealer who'd been caught giving short weight. He hadn't expected Kingstown to have a shop like Munk's with a scale that could weigh his packets. The town council had fined him most of his stock and put him in jail besides. She wondered how the raven and pig had escaped. And why they'd come for her. She frowned.

"You still want to cross the mountains?" said the raven.

"To Iskany?" Dru forgot her troubling questions.

33

"To anywhere you please so long as you get us over the mountains. You can have old Bob and the caravan for your troubles."

Dru sank down on the edge of the trough. The raven darted across the floor to snap up a lost water beetle. The pig stepped forward, jerking his snout at the butter on the floor.

"Better not," Dru told him. "You might eat chips of crock."

She hesitated a second, then reached back for a small cheese. "Here."

The pig took it gently, laid it on the floor and bowed. Dru solemnly bowed back.

"*Drucilla!*"

She stood and looked around frantically. "I have to go!" She feared Willie would be sent to find her.

Humphrey carried the cheese through the door and around the springhouse.

"We must leave tonight," the raven told Dru. "Meet us at the creek where the path goes down from the stable."

Humphrey peered in the door. Dru climbed onto the ledge and unhooked half a dozen tied cheeses hanging from the ceiling.

"Can you carry these to the caravan?"

The pig tapped "yes" and moved back so Dru could toss the cheeses outside. She found another crock of butter, the last, and waited for the raven to walk out the door.

"I can't get out until late," she told him.

34

"We'll wait."

"DRUCILLA!"

"*Coming!*" When she turned from locking the door, bird and pig and one cheese were gone. The hognose lay belly up on the step. She scooped it up and dropped it in her large apron pocket. She'd leave it along the road where nobody would chase it and try to kill it. It curled up in her pocket and lay still.

Dru ran across the yard, pushed past Mrs. Grainger, dropped crock and key on the table and kept going until she reached the attic. She tugged open the hatbox and laid the snake inside. She hesitated over the lid. She didn't want the snake to smother but she didn't want it roaming the inn, either. She compromised, setting the lid on but leaving it unbuckled.

The snake was still there, burrowed under the packets of herbs, when she returned that evening.

Packing didn't take long. She'd outworn or outgrown most of the clothes she'd brought with her. The rest made a pile not much larger than Sally's. Dru set the tin box on top and tied the corners of her shawl around it. She put the bundle beside the hatbox, laid Sally's old cloak on the foot of the bed and sat at the window to wait.

The moon was full. She didn't know if that was a help or a danger. She wondered about the caravan and how the pig and raven had gotten it here. What had happened to the man? And why had the raven asked for Dru?

By the time the inn stilled, she was tempted to undress, crawl into bed and forget mystagogic ravens and calculating pigs. But it was her one chance to reach Iskany and a spell school.

She took up the cloak, the hatbox and the bundle and tiptoed down the stairs. The door at the bottom opened noiselessly but she kept as close as she could to the wall so the hall floor wouldn't creak. The only sound was the scuttling of a mouse as Dru crossed the kitchen.

The bolt on the door had never been oiled. Its grating was supposed to warn of burglars. Dru used the dishrag to rub it with butter as she gently worked it free. The noise it made was slight. Dru moved her belongings through the door and closed it gently behind her.

She stood for a moment, considering. She didn't want to meet Willie snake-hunting or saddle-stealing. Nor did she want to be seen from his room over the stable. She wished she knew an invisibility spell.

She crossed the moonlit yard quickly, keeping close to the woodpile, hurried down the steps and around the springhouse. That put her on the far side of the creek where there was shadow from trees but no path. She stumbled twice, once to her knees, and limped to the elm opposite the stable.

"I'm here," she called softly.

There was an answering grunt and the thrashing of a heavy body. Dru followed the sound and found Humphrey getting to his feet. He whuffed happily at her arm and led the way through the woods. It wasn't until they reached the caravan that Dru realized they'd circled the end of the village. The caravan was just far enough off the Kingstown road to be hidden.

It looked much as it had the first time she'd seen it. The frame of cubbyholes was gone but the door was tied open and the gray horse stood head down between the shafts. Dru peered suspiciously from behind a bush.

"Raven?" she whispered.

"The name's Pitt." He stepped from under the caravan. "What's wrong?"

"Who hitched the horse?"

"Nobody. He hasn't been unhitched since we left Kingstown. That's one of the things we need you for." He cocked his right eye up at Dru. "You can harness a horse?"

"Of course." All she had to do was remember how she took it off. She walked briskly to the caravan door. The floor was almost as high as her waist. "Where are the steps?"

"Kingstown."

Dru frowned. "You must have left in a hurry."

"You going to stand here talking until somebody finds us?"

Dru set her things inside the door, then tossed in the cheeses that had been left in a row on the ground. Humphrey went to watch road. With Pitt squawking directions and Dru at the horse's head, they guided the caravan backward between the trees and onto the moonlit road.

Following Pitt's instructions, Dru found the dismantled stage on racks under the caravan. She used two planks to make a ramp to the door. Humphrey tested it cautiously, then ran up and turned to grunt approval through the door.

"You're right," said Pitt as he followed, "it is easier than steps."

"Don't you ever fly?" said Dru.

"Are you going to put those boards away and get us out of here?"

Dru slid the planks back onto the rack and returned to the door for her cloak. It was too warm a night for it but she didn't want to be recognized when they drove through the village.

As she draped the cloak over her head, Pitt squawked instructions through the door. "And let Humphrey out to look for a campsite as soon as the sky pales. Sooner, if you think we're going to run out of woods."

Dru shut the door and hurried to the front of the caravan, holding the cloak up so she wouldn't trip on it. A metal footstep smaller than her hand was the only help to the driver's seat. At least the seat was padded. She lifted the reins, flicked them cautiously and grinned with delight when the horse stepped forward.

The wheels were well greased. The only sounds were the soft thud of hooves and the chirping of insects and frogs. The houses they passed were dark and looked small from the high seat. Dru felt mysterious and important traveling while everyone slept. The inn gave her a moment of uneasiness but all the windows were still dark and nothing moved except a dog sniffing around the porch steps. It raised its head to watch them pass.

They crossed the road where Sally's aunt lived. Perhaps they'd meet in Summerfalls. If Sally saw the caravan, she'd come asking for another fortune. Dru laughed, imagining the surprise.

They reached the landing and ferry house. Dru turned the horse onto the river road where houses were fewer. After they passed the last one, the road narrowed. Trees met over it, shutting out the moonlight. Dru felt both safer and more nervous. She pushed off the hot cloak and strained eyes and ears at the deep shadows.

The insects and frogs quit their chirping as the caravan approached and took it up again when they'd passed. They moved in a ball of silence. Dru relaxed enough to doze, wakened once by a wheel jolting through a deep hole and again by shrieks inside the caravan.

The horse stopped before Dru could pull the reins. He looked back as she scrambled to the ground.

The pig shrieks stopped. Pitt squawked something about a snake lover. The hognose must have gotten out and crawled over Humphrey in the dark. Dru tugged open the door. Pig and bird were waiting for her.

"I'm sorry," she told Humphrey. It was hard to tell, since a pig's mouth was naturally shaped in a smile, but it seemed Humphrey was laughing.

"That's all right for you," Pitt told him. "But I'm the one almost got trampled on."

Humphrey snortled at him, then grunted a question.

The raven leaned forward to cock an eye at the east. "Yes, I suppose so. You better put the ramp up, snake lover."

"I'm just taking it someplace safe," Dru told him and marched to the rear of the caravan.

She yanked out the planks and slammed them into place. Humphrey walked down, grunting something soothing at her, and went to confer with the horse. Dru put the planks away. She didn't know if she should shut the door or tie it back. She leaned against it, waiting for the bird to give a hint.

"Isn't it early to camp?" she said.

"Best to be safe. Farmers go to market early, others get home late. We only travel a few hours a night."

While Dru was trying to figure how many weeks it would take to reach Summerfalls, the caravan moved. She leaped for the reins, yelling, "Whoa!"

"The door!" squawked Pitt.

The horse stopped and looked back. Dru turned to the door.

"Leave it open," said Pitt.

She tied it and ran to the horse's head. He waited for her to take hold but she didn't lead him. They walked together, following Humphrey's pale rump through the trees. They stopped and Dru fumbled for the harness buckles.

"Will he be all right loose?" she wondered.

40

Humphrey gave an assuring grunt.

Dru hauled the planks out again. While the raven walked down them, she felt inside for her hatbox. It lay on its side, which explained the snake's escape. She groped for the packets, hoping the two she needed hadn't been scattered too far. She found the cumin seed by smell and the salt by feel and taste. She mixed them in her hand.

"Save this abode from harm and hindrance; protect its folk from pilf and peril." Dru circled the caravan, chanting and sprinkling the mixture on the ground. Bushes and branches caught at her and she stumbled. She had to repeat the chant twice to complete the circle.

"Araca dac; avanda ware! By salt and seed I command thee," she finished, closing the circle.

She brushed the last of the mix from her hand and looked up. The three animals stood staring at her. Trying not to look too pleased, she took her cloak from the seat and wrapped it around her with a flourish.

She'd never slept outdoors before but she was even more afraid to grope around the dark caravan. She chose what she thought was a soft stretch of ground and lay down. It wasn't as soft as she'd thought and the woods seemed suddenly full of noise. Then she heard Humphrey and Pitt talking quietly nearby. She pulled the cloak tighter and closed her eyes. When she opened them, it was noon and she was alone.

Patches of sunshine blotched the caravan and its ramp. She kicked free of the cloak and hurried to inspect her home.

41

❧ CHAPTER FIVE ❧

Except for the rumpled bunk across the front, the caravan looked like a storeroom, not a place where somebody lived. The top bunk was filled with carefully made flat wooden boxes. A cupboard had been built on a wall but crates of bottles blocked its doors. A large kettle and some tin trays filled one back corner. In the other, the frame of diamond cubbyholes stood on a battered chest. The cheeses, scattered across the floor, reminded Dru she was hungry.

She unstacked enough crates to open one of the upper cupboard doors. Masses of spiderweb showed how long it had been since the door was last opened. The plates and bowls and cups were tin, dented and very dirty but they were there. Somebody, sometime, had lived in the caravan. Probably the real Dr. Blessing.

Dru took a cup, shut the door and found a knife in the drawer beneath it. She had to restack the crates to reach the cheeses. She took one outside and sat on the top of the the ramp, her back against the side of the door.

The knife was chipped and so dull she nearly stabbed herself sawing the strings from the cheese. She wished she'd thought to take some bread from the pantry.

She wondered if her uncle had sent anyone looking for her. If he didn't offer a reward, nobody would look very long. She guessed the animals were keeping to the woods so if the caravan was found, they'd still be free. She wondered again how and why they'd left Kingstown and how they'd known her name.

The cheese made her thirsty. She found a stream so close behind the caravan it was a wonder she hadn't stepped in it while drawing the protective circle. The horse stood in a clearing on the other side, dozing in the sun and swishing his tail at flies. He paid no attention to Dru when she washed the cup, but while she was drinking, he lifted his head and she heard a wagon pass on the hidden road. The horse's head drooped again. Dru drank a second cup, washed her face and hands in the icy water and dried them on her skirt.

She didn't want to sleep in the messy bunk until she'd washed the bedding, but it was too late in the day for it to dry. She must find an open, sunny space before the weather changed.

She walked along the stream searching for materials to make a broom. Something disturbed the bushes to her right.

"It's too late," said the raven. "I'll never fly."

Dru stopped to listen.

Humphrey snortled.

"But they're almost long enough to clip again," said Pitt. "No, it's the wing muscles. They'll never hold me now."

So that's why the raven never flew. His wing feathers had been clipped each year, probably since he was a fledgling. Poor Pitt. He'd probably never flown.

Humphrey gruntled something.

"No!" Pitt squawked. "No sentimental slobber! We go on just as planned."

Dru wanted to hear more, but the bushes were rustling and she could imagine what Pitt would say if he caught her eavesdropping. She hurried back the way she'd come and took a nap.

She ate cheese for supper and went to get the horse. She wanted to hitch him while she could see the buckles and before the raven came back to watch. The horse helped, backing between the shafts and turning his head when she picked up the wrong strap. There were places where the harness had rubbed him on the journey from Kingstown.

She patted his nose. "I'll be right back."

He nodded but it might have been from the pressure of her hand.

She'd seen plantain where the horse had been grazing. She mashed the large thick leaves in the wooden mortar from the hatbox and tore strips from an old petticoat to make pads to hold the pulp in place and protect from more rubbing. When she replaced the mortar, the snake was back in the hatbox.

44

Dru set the top on and wedged the box between crates so it wouldn't topple no matter how great the jolt. Then she sat on the ramp, her back against the side of the door, and waited. When they came, it was so dark that Humphrey was a blur and she didn't see Pitt until he stood on the planks.

"We have to talk," she told him.

"Don't spread any more junk around the caravan," he told her. "Bob went around licking it up. Horses aren't sensible about eating and drinking."

Dru looked around, concerned. "He didn't get sick, did he?"

"No thanks to you. Humphrey went around eating most of it. All that salt doesn't set too well."

"Poor Humphrey." Dru scratched the pig behind the ears. He rumbled contentedly.

"Poor snake, poor Humphrey," mimicked Pitt.

"And poor me," Dru told him. "What am I supposed to eat? Those cheeses won't last to Summerfalls at the rate we travel."

"I told you, we can't risk being seen."

"We could if we painted the caravan."

"Where will you get the money for paint? Work another spell?"

Humphrey lifted his head from Dru's lap to suggest something.

"Is that a spell you put on Bob?" said Pitt.

From the way Humphrey sighed, Dru guessed Pitt hadn't answered what he'd been asked.

45

"That's just medicine," she told them. "He was chafed from being hitched so long but it won't need a spell to make it heal."

The raven cocked his head. "You know a lot of spells?"

"Some." Dru thought he was going to ask for one to help him fly and decided to warn him. She told about closing the inn without getting to Harvest Fair and about stopping a boat but getting Willie instead of royalty. "And New Year's Eve I worked a Prosperity spell for Sally and now she's gone off to Summerfalls in her new clothes. All my spells work the wrong way."

"That last one worked right."

"Not for me!" Sally's leaving was too new, too painful. Dru blinked and ran her sleeve under her nose. Humphrey made comforting noises.

"But your spells do work," Pitt insisted. "You could sell them."

"You can't make spells up in batches like fortunes!"

"Ever try?"

"Of course not!"

"There you are." Dru opened her mouth to protest but Pitt added, "That why you want to go to Iskany? Because of the spells?"

"Of course." The raven had made her angry instead of lonely. She lifted her chin. "Where else can I learn about spells? I'm going to be a sorcerer."

"Never heard of those spell schools taking in anyone from outside Iskany."

46

"Have you ever been to Iskany?" From the way he avoided questions about it, Dru was sure he hadn't. She waited eagerly for him to admit it so she could say, There you are.

But the raven said, "Humphrey was born and trained there. Humphrey, did you ever hear . . . ."

Dru interrupted. "I know somebody in Farewell who can help me."

She didn't want to hear Humphrey's tapped yes or no. But she couldn't help wondering if Farewell had a town council and where they'd send her if the spell school . . . she didn't want to think about that. Instead, she told Humphrey and Pitt about her mother and old Munk and the spell book he'd given her.

"And his son has a shop in Farewell near a spell school." The words came out slowly. She was remembering when the animals had returned to the inn. They'd been looking for someone named Dru. She stopped scratching Humphrey's ear. "But you know Munk, don't you? He sent you to me."

Pitt squawked, "You going to sit here blathering all night?"

Dru laughed. She was beginning to learn more from the questions Pitt wouldn't answer than from those he did.

"Come on, Humphrey." Pitt led the way into the caravan.

Dru prepared for travel. They were farther off the road than the night before but in a clearing large enough

47

for a careful turn. She drove out slowly, stopping Bob a few yards from the road so she could walk to the edge and listen in both directions. She climbed back up and tugged the rein on the side toward Summerfalls.

She wasn't sure how much direction Bob needed but she knew he needed some. Humphrey must have guided him from Kingstown to the inn. Dru was beginning to understand what a terrible journey that had been for them, traveling a few hours each night, hiding all day and always fearful of being discovered. Without steps or Dru's makeshift ramp, neither Pitt nor Humphrey could get into the caravan. They'd walked all the way.

If Humphrey lay down, Pitt could walk onto his back and ride, but Dru knew the bird was too proud to do that and too sensitive about not flying. Poor Pitt. She pitied him most of all.

She was glad Munk had sent the animals to her. She would never have dared try the journey alone. She just wished they'd come while Sally was still at the inn. They could have gone to Iskany together, the way they'd planned.

Dru sighed. Sally would know how to get Pitt to stop for food. But there still wouldn't be money to pay for it, just the few pennies in the tin box. She'd probably ask Dru to work a money-making spell. Dru grinned, wondering what she'd have to use. Goldenrod? Baldmoney? She'd probably find pennyroyal in the mountains.

She sat up straight. The tightening of the reins stopped the horse.

"Sorry," she murmured and got him moving again.

Pitt squawked inside, demanding to know what was wrong.

Dru found a panel and slid it open. The boxes on the top bunk blocked it but she shouted through, "It's all right. Just a mistake."

She shut the panel so she couldn't hear Pitt complaining to Humphrey. She didn't want any distraction from her sudden thought.

She'd gather herbs and sell them. There was probably a sorcerers' shop in Summerfalls, at least during the summer, but there'd be none in the villages they'd pass. People would be glad to buy herbs that had been properly gathered and prepared. She could even spellbind them to order. Not the complicated ones, not until she'd been trained and could make them work the right way. But there was no harm in working Safe Journey or Pleasant Dream spells. She pictured the caravan clean and cozy with bunches of cloth-covered herbs hanging from the ceiling.

After that, her days took on a new order. She ate after they camped, waiting for first light so she could search for herbs. Pennyroyal and bergamot were plentiful and sometimes she found bloodroot. One stream had watercress which she ate between slices of cheese. After gathering herbs, she chose a patch of ground near the caravan and spread her cloak.

She despaired of ever sleeping in the bunk. The only morning they stopped in a clearing large enough to

49

spread the bedding, the stream was too shallow to wash it in.

What was left of the day after she woke she spent cleaning the caravan. It was slow. She knew without asking that Pitt and Humphrey wouldn't allow a fire even in daytime to heat water. The contents of the cupboard had to be carried to a stream, washed, dried in patches of sun and carried back to shelves wiped clean with pieces of the old torn petticoat.

The two cupboard drawers were jammed with fascinating and useful oddments. She was relieved to find twine to tie the herbs. She couldn't spare another petticoat.

The chest held old costumes. They were too large for Dru but she spent a whole afternoon dressing up and posing in front of a streaked mirror hanging behind the cubbyhole frame.

The beautifully carved boxes on the top bunk puzzled her. They were filled with gears and cogs that moved busily when a handle was turned but produced nothing from the slots on the ends. When she asked about them that evening, Humphrey chuckled.

"Money-making machines," Pitt told her.

Dru stopped scratching Humphrey's ears. "Really?"

Humphrey's snort said no. The pig made a speech Dru couldn't follow, though she'd begun to understand him. Not the way Pitt did but she could sense his feelings and intent by the way he shaded his grunts and snortles. And when she did need Pitt's help, she could tell if the raven translated truly. He did this time, with much urging and correction from Humphrey.

Neither Pitt nor Humphrey was sure how the trick worked, but the cogs and gears were to impress and to hide the real workings underneath, an arrangement of coils. Paper money was wound inside one coil ahead of time. Then when plain paper was wound into one slot, the money unwound out of the slot on the other end.

Dru shook her head. "Nobody would believe it. Who'd sell a money-making machine that really worked?"

"You say you need lots of money in a hurry. Somebody's sick or something. But the machine is spellbound to make only one bill each midnight. You can wind two or three bills in there ahead of time so the buyer can take the machine home and try it by himself one midnight."

Dru grinned. "And if he tries to make more, it just proves the spell. How many did he sell?"

Humphrey sighed.

"Not many," Pitt told her.

The trouble was finding buyers. The man had stopped at local inns to learn who the local rich people were. If one of them bought Elixir, the bottle given them had an extra ring around the neck, Pitt's signal to give them a gold-tied fortune.

"Befriend a dark stranger and reap rewards," Dru remembered. "But I'm not rich and I didn't buy any Elixir."

"You wanted to go to Iskany."

"But how did you know you'd come back?"

"We had plans."

"And you knew Munk."

"No."

Humphrey corrected him.

"We knew he was in Kingstown," Pitt said. "Dr. Blessing, the real Dr. Blessing, knew him in Iskany before he came to Zuus."

"And so Munk helped you."

The raven stretched his wings and cocked his eye at the patch of the sky over the caravan. It was too early to be on the road. He grumbled about prying people but Humphrey coaxed and Dru questioned and little by little the story was told.

The real Dr. Blessing had trained Humphrey and a crow. Traveling with him had been different. They'd never left towns in the middle of the night and they'd always had plenty to eat. Pitt sounded skeptical but Humphrey insisted it was true. But Dr. Blessing had died suddenly, far from Iskany, and just as suddenly another man had taken Humphrey and the caravan in charge.

"What happened to the crow?" said Dru and was immediately sorry. Even Humphrey was distressed. Of course, the crow had flown, abandoning Humphrey and teaching the man to get a bird with clipped feathers. Poor Pitt, Dru thought, not daring to say it.

Pitt ignored her question and the chance to gain sympathy with tales of injustice and mistreatment.

He said, "Sooner or later that cheat was going to be caught and somebody else would steal us the way he did Humphrey. So we decided to steal ourselves soon as we found somebody to help us over the mountains. Humphrey knows a place in Iskany where we can live and be safe, but we're never going to get there if you don't get working."

He walked up the ramp past Dru. She started to block him with her arm, then remembered how sensitive he was about not flying.

She just asked, "What happened to the man?" and hoped he'd answer.

From inside the caravan, Pitt said, "Tried to sell a money-making machine in Kingstown and somebody told Lord Farnum how it worked."

Munk, Dru guessed, who'd been told by Pitt about the machine.

Humphrey grunted in surprise. A dark line glided up the ramp past Dru. Pitt squawked in rage. Humphrey chuckled.

Dru scrambled into the caravan but the hognose was safely curled in the bottom of the hatbox, lumpy with toad. Every morning Dru laid the hatbox gently on its side near the door. When she woke in the afternoon, it was empty but the snake returned to it as faithfully as it had to the step by the springhouse. It usually returned before dusk and Dru had thought this time it had left for good. But it had only been waiting for Pitt to move off the ramp.

"It likes us," she told Pitt. She put on the lid and

wedged the box securely between the crates.

"The agreement was for you," Pitt said. "It doesn't include every 'poor thing' you find along the way."

Humphrey entered, snortling soothingly, and lay down. Pitt stood in the curve of his neck, braced against the sway of the caravan. It was their usual traveling position.

Dru put away the plank ramp and shut the door. That and unhitching Bob were all she could do for the animals. If some unscrupulous man took a notion to become Dr. Blessing Number Three, Dru couldn't stop him.

No wonder Pitt and Humphrey hid in the woods all day, though Dru didn't think that would save them. A wolf or lynx would catch Pitt and some farmer would find Humphrey. For the first time, Dru shared their fear of being seen. She listened long and carefully before letting Bob onto the road. Then she drew the cloak over her head and considered the problem.

Painting the caravan was the only thing that would help but she couldn't get money for paint without being seen. If she went door to door selling herbs, there'd be questions. Everybody in the little villages was known. They'd try to find out where she'd come from and the caravan would be found.

Some farmer would buy the kettle and the trays the Elixir had been made in, but Dru couldn't get them to a farm without using the caravan that had to be painted first. Her thoughts went in circles until Bob turned a corner and startled her from her brooding.

She raised up enough to look back over the caravan's roof but Bob hadn't decided to take another way. There was no other way he could have gone. The road had made a sharp turn toward the river.

The sky behind them showed no stars. Clouds, thought Dru, and turned forward, frowning. Bob walked into fog that swirled around his hooves. It rose as they entered a village and was belly high on the horse when he stopped at the end of the road.

Dru slid back the panel and bent to call softly, "Pitt, we have a problem."

❧ CHAPTER SIX ❧

"There is no other way," said Dru. "It's the ferry or back the way we came."

They went back. But only far enough to find a camping place. Dru left Bob hitched until they decided what to do.

"We have to cross," Pitt said. "But when's safest?"

Humphrey grunted a question.

"Trade him a bottle of Elixir." He meant the ferryman.

"I have some money." Dru hoped the few coins Sally had left her would be enough. "We don't want to call attention to ourselves. I mean, no more than we have to."

Pitt and Humphrey agreed. It took Dru longer to convince them they couldn't leave after dark. The ferryman would probably refuse to take them across. They decided to cross just before dusk became dark. There'd be fewer people about and they'd have all night to travel up the other side of the river and escape the curiosity of anyone who did see or hear about them at the ferry crossing.

The dark sky worried Dru but she shuddered at the thought of the messy bunk. She'd sleep on the floor, but with the boxes and kettle and crates, there wasn't room for both Dru and Humphrey to lie down.

She put as much of herself under the ramp as she could and not just for protection from rain. It was going to be dark a long time and she wanted the comfort of Humphrey's grunts and snortles and Pitt's harsh voice. She couldn't hear the words but it sounded like an argument. If it was, she fell asleep before they settled it.

She woke in a small white world, her hair wet and her cloak damp from the fog. The animals were gone. She climbed into the caravan and sat shivering on the floor, waiting for the fog to lift. She laid the unlidded hatbox by the door but, like Dru, the snake was too chilled to stir until the sun burned away the fog. Then Dru took her breakfast cheese outside and stared in amazement.

What had darkened the night sky wasn't cloud but mountains. She'd seen their tops, higher each day above the trees, but suddenly this wall of rock was cutting off the sky, reaching toward the river and forcing the road to the other side. Dru was glad they could pass the mountains.

Instead of gathering herbs, she made a broom. The materials she found were no better than those she'd passed over but last night had been a reminder that the good weather couldn't last. She had to stop wandering in the woods and wading in the streams (lollygagging, Mrs. Grainger would call it, and she'd be right) and finish cleaning the caravan.

The sun was overhead and the grass dry when she finished the broom. She tested it on the ramp. As she'd expected, the twigs were too coarse to sweep well but she'd swept enough cobwebs off ceiling corners in the inn to know what to do about it. The handle was crooked and the twigs not neatly tied but Dru was pleased with her handiwork.

She added tiny wild onions to her lunch cheese and leafed through her spell book while she ate. Then she slid the crates down the ramp and restacked them under elderberry bushes that were just beginning to bloom. They had traveled higher in the mountains than Dru had thought.

She moved everything except the cupboard, chest and bunks outside. She'd already brought pots of water from the tiny stream. She tied a square of torn petticoat over the broom, sprinkled it with water and swept the caravan's ceiling. The dust and cobwebs were too thick for the wet cloth to hold them all. Some fell on Dru's head, along with dried leaves and dead bugs. She tied another strip of petticoat over her hair and cleaned the rear wall so she could open that door, too.

The top and bottom were separate, with their own latches and bolts. They opened inward and were usually blocked by the crates, kettle and trays.

She changed the cloth on her broom, rinsing the dirty one and spreading it on the grass next to her drying cloak. She was sweeping around the built-in cupboard when the light dimmed and Pitt squawked, "What are you doing?"

Dru turned and propped the broom on the floor like a flagstaff. "Cleaning. Doesn't it look better?"

"No." He ducked so Humphrey could walk over him.

The pig grunted to Dru and pointed his snout at the bunks.

"Traitor!" squawked Pitt.

Dru knelt and peered under the bunk. She found three more money-making machines but they couldn't be what Humphrey meant. Dru moved them to the lower bunk while Pitt screeched and flapped his wings so that she was grateful he couldn't fly and Humphrey could block his darts and dashes. The pig was surprisingly quick.

Dru poked the broom under the bunk until it touched wall, and swept. The broom brought out hay, rolls of dust, a spool of dirty thread and two small coins.

"Traitor," Pitt said again but in his normal harsh voice.

Humphrey sat down and talked sense to him. Pitt lifted the coins from the dust and laid them on a cleaner patch of floor. Dru kept sweeping until the floor under the bunk was clean. By then Pitt had a small pile of coins, all sizes and from at least three of the five kingdoms.

"My retirement fund," he told Dru.

"Can't you find a safer place?"

"It was safe enough until you came along."

She didn't remind him that she'd been asked to come along. "Are they all there? Would you like a cup to keep them in?"

Pitt raised his left eye toward her. "You're letting me keep them?"

"They're yours, aren't they? Do you want a cup or a bowl?"

She started to get up but Pitt said, "Neither. I stick them in cracks by the wall."

Dru nodded. "I'll warn you next time I clean under there."

Pitt's left eye stared up at her. He took up a coin and, still watching Dru, ducked under the bunk, wings slightly raised for balance. He popped out and grabbed another, still keeping an eye on Dru. When he came out again, Dru said, "Of course, you may not have a retirement if we don't get over the mountains."

Humphrey gave a just-what-I've-been-telling-you grunt. Dru guessed it was what they'd been arguing about the night before.

Pitt dropped a coin to squawk, "I'm not paying for paint that goes on somebody else's caravan."

Humphrey objected but Dru said, "You're right."

Pitt dropped the coin again, this time in surprise. It rolled toward the cupboard. As Pitt chased it, Dru said, "But if you lend me money to buy paint, I'll be able to sell herbs and repay you."

Pitt took the coin under the bunk without answering.

When he came out, Humphrey was sitting on the rest of the money.

"All right, all right," Pitt told him. "I'll lend her the money, not that I'm likely to see it again."

Humphrey didn't move. He grunted something that started a three-way argument about who should pay for the ferry. Pitt lost. He made mourning sounds as Dru counted out the coins.

"Take big ones so you don't take so many," he told her.

She also tried to take the less shiny ones but she didn't have much choice. Nobody in the villages would take foreign coins and when she'd sorted out those from Zuus, half of them pennies, Dru knew there wasn't enough to buy paint even before paying the ferryman. But she refused Pitt's suggestion that she return some of the money.

"We'll have to take more than one ferry," she told him. "Summerfalls is on this side of the river."

She dropped the coins in her pocket and followed the animals outside to change the cover on her broom. Cleaning didn't require the attention herb-gathering did. There was always something new and interesting to see or learn in the woods or along the stream banks. Sweeping, though, left her mind free to worry about crossing the river.

Dru wished again for Sally. With two of them on the driver's seat, there'd be less chance of someone trying to take the caravan. Maybe she should dress Humphrey in one of the fancy costumes from the chest. She stopped grinning and frowned, leaning on the broom as she thought.

She glanced at the sun and decided the caravan was as clean as she could get it without hot soapy water and a scrub brush. She pulled the cloth from her head and went to call the animals. As she'd suspected, they were nearby. She sat on a crate under the elderberry bushes and told them her plan. From the way they looked at each other, she realized they'd been worried, too.

They retreated to the woods, Humphrey moving more quietly than Pitt, while Dru hurried to move things back into the caravan. She fumed as she worked.

Pitt was going to have to talk through the open panel so his voice would seem to come from Humphrey on the driver's seat. But not a word had been said about how he'd get to the upper bunk. Dru had felt too awkward about bringing it up and Pitt had ignored the problem, turning over a rock to search for grubs. Why didn't he admit what they all knew? Then Dru could just lift him up. But no, he expected her to find some pride-saving way to get him up there.

She stopped halfway up the ramp, the last two money-making machines in her arms. Maybe Pitt had practiced enough to strengthen his wings. Maybe he could fly now. She walked slowly into the caravan and dropped the boxes she carried on top of the stack. If Pitt could fly, he could go anywhere. Like that crow of Dr. Blessing's that never came back.

She took a scrap of petticoat and started toward the stream to wash. Pitt's squawk stopped her.

"You forgot these!" He was standing with Humphrey beside the crates. He must be really upset to call across the clearing like that.

Dru turned back. "I didn't forget them."

"You can't leave them. This Elixir's valuable!"

Maybe she could sell it with her herbs. "Does it work?"

Humphrey chortled.

"Never stayed long enough to find out," said Pitt.

Humphrey added something; Pitt translated. "It isn't what Dr. Blessing made."

"Then I can't sell it," Dru said firmly and started for the stream.

Pitt called her back. "The crates could be useful."

Dru nodded.

"If you're keeping the crates, might as well leave the bottles in them."

"The bottles are the heaviest part."

"Poor horse," mimicked Pitt.

"Poor me," Dru told him. "I'll have to move them every time I clean."

"Nobody wants your cleaning."

Humphrey disagreed.

Dru added, "Besides, we need the room."

"So you can collect more 'poor things'? We have too many now."

But she was already lifting bottles from the top crates

and stacking them neatly under the elderberry bushes. Then she remembered Humphrey drinking a bottle during the show on the green. Dru had already sampled the Elixir. It tasted terrible but maybe the pig liked it. She asked and had no trouble understanding the answer.

"Humphrey drank colored water," Pitt explained.

Dru could understand why.

"Elixir's too valuable to waste," Pitt went on.

Dru ignored the hint and kept stacking bottles. Pitt squawked again when he realized she was only going to unpack half the crates.

"We don't have room for two stacks now," she told him. "I had to take all the money-making machines off the top bunk so they wouldn't crush you if they slid."

She waited, giving him another chance to say something about getting up there, but he just stalked off into the underbrush. Dru sighed and lifted an empty crate.

Humphrey stayed to help. Dru set the crates on the end of the ramp and the pig pushed them into the caravan. Dru had only to restack them where the trays and kettle had stood. She shoved the money-making machines tight against them. The rear door was still blocked, but although the carved boxes took up as much floor space as a stack of crates, they were only half as high. Dru could open the top part of the door whenever she wanted.

Humphrey followed her to the rear of the caravan. The anxious way he watched her pull another plank out and carry it inside convinced her that Pitt couldn't fly yet. She made a ramp to the upper bunk but the only place she could brace the bottom end of the plank was against the base of the cupboard. The distance was too short for a gentle slope.

Humphrey sighed.

"It is awfully steep," Dru agreed. "You better have Pitt try it."

So she wouldn't embarrass the raven by watching, she hurried down to the stream and took her time washing. When she returned, Pitt had mastered the steep ramp. He ran up it full speed, flapping his wings as his claws scrabbled for rough spots in the plank. He perched on the bunk rail and settled his wings. Dru had given him the very thing he needed to strengthen them. He'd probably run up and down the plank all night.

Dru forced down her evening ration of cheese, gave the rind to Humphrey and searched the spell book again. The most suitable spell was Protection of Livestock on Crossing, meant for fording rivers. But the way her spells worked, probably everyone would get across except her.

She settled for two of the Safe Journey spells made of comfrey, one hung from Bob's harness, the other from the railing on the upper bunk. And since crossing on a ferry was a business transaction, she wiped a Good Business spell of bloodroot tea on both doorsills and the floor in front of the driver's seat.

"I hope you aren't planning to wash the whole floor," Pitt told her. "It's dark already."

It wasn't, but Dru hurried her preparations. The problem was getting Humphrey to the driver's seat. The planks were too short for the distance. Though it wasn't as steep as Pitt's ramp, Humphrey was heavier and had no claws to help. His hooves kept slipping and he squealed in frustration. Dru finally sat with her back against his rump and scrooched backward up the ramp, holding the edges of the planks to help push herself along. At last Humphrey scrambled onto the floor in front of the seat.

The caravan creaked. Bob's head jerked up in alarm.

"It's all right," Dru soothed him. "It's just for a little while."

When the planks were stowed away, she draped a blanket over Humphrey's body and her shawl over his head to make a deep hood. If she didn't get closer than the horse's head, he looked like a short, stocky man bundled and hunched against the chill and damp. The illusion would be even better when it was darker.

"Say something," she called.

Pitt obliged in a voice she'd never heard, young and rough but kind. "Get up, sis. Got to get going." In his usual shrill voice, Pitt added, "Going to get us stuck here another day?"

"People move a little when they talk," Dru told Humphrey. "Not that much! You'll lose your shawl."

She adjusted it, wrapped herself in her cloak and squeezed onto the driver's seat. Humphrey was sitting as close to the middle as he could. It balanced better for the horse but that wasn't the reason he was crowding Dru. She could feel him trembling.

"You'll get used to it," she told him softly. Then, with more confidence than she felt, she said, "Ready?"

Humphrey grunted weakly.

Through the open panel, Pitt grumbled, "Would it make any difference if we weren't?"

Dru pulled her cloak over her head, picked up the reins and flicked them. Bob moved forward, but slower and without his usual confidence. Dru worried, but once on the road he seemed to adjust to the change. They passed the turn in the road and approached the village. Dru pushed the reins through Humphrey's blanket at the proper height and hoped they wouldn't fall out and that Bob would stop where he had before, at the ferry.

He did. It had been dark under the trees and only a little lighter in the village but over the river it was light enough to see the opposite shore. Dru patted Humphrey's shoulder and clambered down to knock on the ferry-house door.

She could smell the ferry keeper's supper and hoped he wasn't already eating. He'd probably make them wait until he finished, and three village boys had already gathered to stare at the caravan.

"Can we see the magic pig, missus?" said one.

Another flapped his arms and cried, "Oink! Oink!" to the others' amusement.

The ferryman opened the door and glared at them. He glared at Dru, too, and told her she was too late.

"But my father's ill." Dru tried to make her voice tearful. "We must get to the mountains right away or he'll die."

"You have to spend the night somewhere. It might as well be here."

Dru shook her head. "My brother and I take turns driving. We don't stop. Please, sir, my father is very sick."

The ferryman agreed to be merciful for three times his usual fare. To Dru's alarm, Pitt began haggling in the rough young voice he used for Humphrey. The pig remembered to move just a little when he was supposed to be talking. Dru was surprised at how real he looked. But she didn't want to test the disguise too long or at close quarters.

When the man dropped his price a third, Dru said, "Thank you," and paid him, half expecting a squawk of outrage from the caravan.

The boys followed to the ferry, cawing and oinking and giggling. Dru stayed afoot to answer the man's questions and keep him as far from Humphrey as she could.

As soon as they were away from the bank, he asked, "Which one is Dr. Blessing?"

"Neither," said Dru. "We bought the caravan as is for my father."

She countered with questions of her own. The mountains, she learned, came down to the river in cliffs, first on one side of the river, then the other. There were two

68

more ferries before the one to Summerfalls, which explained why people took boats.

"That ferry's a good mile this side of Summerfalls," the ferryman told her. "The river's too shallow after that for boats. Everything's got to be hauled from the landing into Summerfalls."

No wonder only the wealthy went to Summerfalls. The man was pleased to display his river knowledge and it lasted until they docked. The caravan's rear wheels were scarcely off the plank deck before the ferryman pushed away, no longer curious enough about them to delay getting back to his supper.

After passing half a dozen small buildings, all lamplit or dark, the road turned upriver.

"We clear?" Pitt asked.

Dru answered, "Yes."

"Move over, Humphrey. I want to sit in the middle."

Humphrey's grunt was a definite no.

"But we'll have to talk around you."

Humphrey refused to move. Pitt stayed on the upper bunk and talked through the opening. Though it was the longest night's journey they'd made, it passed like the shortest.

The mountains crowded close to the river. There were no villages on this side and the few farms were widely spaced. Trees were fewer, too, but rocks, some as big as houses, had spilled down the mountainsides. There were hidden campsites among them but Humphrey had to search a long time to find ones the caravan

69

could reach. Once they camped after only a few miles, afraid they'd find nothing else before dawn.

But sunny rocks were even better than meadows for drying laundry. Dru washed the bedding from both bunks and the mattress cover from the bottom one. She threw away the crumbled cornhusk stuffing and refilled it with the dry grass that had packed the Elixir. Each day she set two crates outside for table and bench.

"We'll have lace cloths and tea sets next," Pitt grumbled.

Dru ignored him. The campsites looked homey and the dry cheese seemed to taste better from a tin plate on a crate table. But she was on the last chunk and worried.

"We have to stop at a farm," she told Humphrey and Pitt. "I can't even find wild onions up here."

The animals had been looking longer for food, too. Perhaps that was why Pitt didn't argue very long. His only condition was that they wait until the next ferry so they could cross the river and be up the road before dawn. Dru agreed and sliced the cheese even thinner.

❧ CHAPTER SEVEN ❧

The day they waited to cross the river was cloudy and threatening rain. Dru wished for a fire. Everything was damp and her cloak didn't keep out the chill.

Getting Humphrey into the driver's seat seemed twice as hard as before. Dru was exhausted and almost wished aloud for a Flying spell.

It was drizzling when they reached a farmhouse. Dru's mouth watered at the smells coming from the kitchen. The farmer was pulling off his boots on the porch. He stamped them back on and came to meet the caravan.

"Hey," he called to Humphrey, "I'd sure like to see that calculating pig."

"Don't have it," Pitt said through the open panel.

Dru scrambled down to intercept the man and maneuver him away from Humphrey, explaining about her brother buying the caravan so they could take their sick father to the mountains.

"But we've run short of food. We have things to trade." As she opened the caravan door, Pitt grumbled in an old man's voice. Dru told him, "It's just me, Dad. Go back to sleep."

The iron kettle and trays were ready at the door.

"Got no use for a kettle," the farmer said. Nor did his wife, who'd come onto the porch. "But I'll trade for those trays."

Dru accepted bread, butter, honey, dried beef and more cheese. She refused eggs, not sure how Pitt would feel about them, but took a large crock of milk.

From the way the farmer eyed Humphrey, he was wondering why a brother let his sister slop around doing the lugging. Dru thought of saying he'd hurt his foot, but offering an explanation was more suspicious than acting as if everything were normal.

Because of the bad weather, it was darker than they'd planned when they reached the ferry landing. Dru wondered if the ferryman would see the signal but they'd barely settled to wait when the flatboat arrived, delivering a farmer home from the village across the river.

He halted his wagon beside Dru to say, "If you're putting on a show, I'll go back with you."

"We're just passing through," Dru told him.

"You're lucky I was bringing a regular," the ferryman told them. "I wouldn't come out in this for the signal."

"What's the fare?" Pitt asked, as if they had a choice.

The price quoted was enough for a round trip but Dru paid, ignoring Pitt's grumbling. She led Bob aboard and stayed by his head, keeping the ferryman's attention. When he asked about the pig and crow, she explained again about buying the caravan.

The drizzle turned to rain before they docked but that didn't keep half a dozen youngsters from following them through the village.

"Didn't get this much attention when we were selling Elixir and wanted it," Pitt grumbled.

"It must be the Good Business spell," said Dru.

Pitt made an unbelieving noise. "Then why didn't it get us lower fares?"

"I told you, my spells work in wrong ways."

Bob turned upriver and Dru had to bow her head to keep the rain from hitting her face. The road was uphill and muddy and a strain on the horse. He stopped twice to rest. The third time, Humphrey let Dru know it was time to camp. Pitt objected but was ignored since he was the only one not wet.

While she wrestled with the planks, one of Dru's shoes stuck in the mud. Before she got her foot back in, it had collected a film of water. Then Humphrey's hooves slipped on the wet planks and he slid down shrieking, landing them both in the mud.

"Who's there? What happened?" squawked Pitt.

"Come out and see," Dru dared him.

She scraped most of the mud off with her hands and lost her shoe again putting the planks under the caravan. She huddled against the caravan's sheltered side and thought longingly of the attic room at the inn, then of the cottage she'd shared with her mother. She was feel-

73

ing miserable inside as well as out when Humphrey returned to lead them to a campsite.

The rain had washed him clean but Dru dried him with an old velvet robe from the chest (after she'd used one side to scrub herself). She gave him some of the fresh bread and milk, mixed in a tin bowl, and chopped some of the dried beef for Pitt. She wished she had oats for Bob, though she didn't know how he'd eat them in the rain.

As a candle stub burned, they talked about the farmer and the crossing. Dru could laugh about the fall in the mud but she didn't think it was as funny as Pitt did. She lay on the bunk listening to the rain on the roof, Humphrey's sleep grunts and Pitt's dream mutterings. She was smiling when she fell asleep.

The clouds lifted late the next morning. Dru stared in amazement at the mountains. They seemed to have grown in the rain like mushrooms, blocking out much of the sky. She could even see those across the river, which must be much narrower here. That pleased Pitt; the next two ferries would cost less. He told Dru the mountains they had to cross were behind these and much higher.

"Poor Bob," she murmured.

Pitt made a disgusted noise and stalked off to forage for food. The animals had stayed in the caravan until the rain stopped. Pitt had spent the time running up and down the plank ramp. To work off energy, he said, but Dru thought he'd be flying soon. She wondered if Humphrey was also remembering the crow who'd flown away and never come back.

74

Using tools found in the cupboard, Dru knocked apart two crates. She'd noticed cross strips nailed to ramps leading to the farmer's chicken house and wanted to try them on the planks Humphrey used to reach the driver's seat. They should keep his hooves from slipping. She cut and hammered, the noise echoing from the huge rocks.

From somewhere among them, Pitt called, "You want everyone from here to the next ferry to hear you?"

"I'm almost finished," Dru called back.

Two more cross pieces and she was. She called Humphrey to test it. The pig still needed steadying from behind but the climb wasn't the struggle it had been and he wouldn't slip again coming down.

He grunted his thanks.

"Glad to do it," Dru told him. She hadn't known she could.

While she admired her handiwork, Humphrey checked the road to see if it was dry enough for travel. He snortled a yes to her and went to tell Pitt. Dru glanced at the sun and hurried to get ready.

Four evenings later they took the ferry to the landing below Summerfalls. It cost more, not less, than the other three. All of Pitt's Zuus coins were gone and all but one of those Sally had left in the tin box.

They'd planned to pull off the road and wait until midnight to pass through Summerfalls, but there was barely room for the road between the cliff and the river. And there was enough traffic so that Dru didn't dare stop. Then they rounded a turn and the cliff was gone, or at least farther back from the road and sloping enough to build on. At the foot of the slope was enough level land for two or three streets, all of them as bright and busy as if it were midday.

"It's like a fair," said Dru. "A great summer-long fair."

But instead of tents and platforms set against caravans, the streets were lined with rows of booths and business establishments. A few carts sold produce or finger food. Jugglers, puppeteers and other entertainers worked on rugs spread at intersections. But most business was done from wooden booths, theaters and restaurants rented for the season.

Customers for all this business lived along streets that crisscrossed the steep mountainside. The higher the house or hotel, the richer its residents. Torches lining the streets and terraces made the mountainside look like a wall of stars.

Dru was so busy gawking and wondering how she could find Sally that she forgot their danger until Pitt used his old man's voice to remind her.

"I can't help it," she told him.

All three of the lower streets were filled with noise and confusion. And light. Dru glanced at Humphrey. The shawl still covered his snout. Dru pulled her own hood down as far as she could. It blocked her view to the sides but if Sally was in the crowd it would be easier for her to see the caravan than for Dru to see her. And if Sally saw them, she'd follow with a penny for another fortune.

"Why don't you hire trumpeters and a herald and parade us through at noon?" grumbled Pitt. He was so worried he'd forgotten to use his old man's voice.

Dru tried to reassure him. From what she could see, nobody paid attention to the shabby caravan unless it got in the way. Then it was only to curse and maybe shove at Bob. Dru had taken the reins back from Humphrey after they'd left the ferry but she made no attempt to guide the horse. He did better finding his own way through the crowd. But progress was so slow Dru began to worry, too, and wished she could see more than what was straight ahead.

The ledge of level ground narrowed, squeezing the three streets into two, then one, less well lit and busy. Then the last booth and torch were left behind but not the shouts and laughter and singsong chants of the sellers.

When they'd gone half a mile without meeting anyone, Dru stopped the caravan and let Humphrey down. When he finally returned, he led Bob a long rough way up the mountainside. Dru could still hear the noise of lower Summerfalls but Humphrey insisted they were safe.

Pitt, after his morning practice flight, agreed. The raven could fly from tree to tree if they weren't too tall or far apart. He guided Dru to the end of the highest street when she set off with her hatbox to sell herbs.

"You can't get lost," he told her. "Walk along the mountain till you reach the stream, then follow it down to the camp."

He must have watched for her return. He and Humphrey met her upstream from the camp. It made her feel a little better and she managed a smile and thank you. The animals followed her silently back to camp. Even Bob seemed anxious. He came to stand behind them as they settled at the edge of the stream.

Dru pulled off her shoes and put her feet in the water. She'd knocked on every kitchen door on four steep and stony streets. Humphrey sat beside her.

On her other side, Pitt said, "Well?"

" 'Not interested,' and bang, shut the door," Dru told him. "They don't even let me explain."

"You don't explain; you show them."

Dru opened the hatbox beside her. "But I . . . ."

"No, no! Show them *you*'re special, different. So they'll know what you're selling is special. Why do you think Dr. Blessing trained Humphrey and that crow? The stuff he made was good but he couldn't sell it 'less he got their attention, showed he had something special."

Humphrey stood and jigged a few steps, kicking up smooth river stones.

"Dance?" said Dru.

Pitt cocked an eye at her. "Can you?"

"No."

"Then something else." He lifted his beak to the tree branches in his attitude of thought.

Dru rubbed her feet. The icy water was making them numb. Maybe she could carry Pitt on her shoulder, screeching insults. That would certainly attract attention. But the bird was longer than her arm. She doubted she could carry him more than a few steps even if he agreed, and she wasn't sure he would.

Humphrey grunted. The hognose snake had tried to sneak behind him to the hatbox. It rose and hissed and shook its tail.

"Right," said Pitt. "Take your poor friend."

Dru tipped the hatbox so it could glide in. "I don't think it would like all the people."

"Good. Then maybe it won't come back."

Humphrey made another suggestion. Pitt translated, inspecting Dru with his left eye. "Wear something from the chest. Something to make you . . . what?" That was to Humphrey who'd interrupted. "Exotic?" said Pitt and made the throat rattle he used for a laugh.

It was only the size of the cheese after supper that convinced Dru to try. The costume they chose was what Dru had thought was a bundle of old curtains but Humphrey showed her openings for head and arms. Layers of fine cloth covered her from neck to ankles. There was an attached scarf to be tossed over the other shoulder or drawn up to cover the face.

"That's better," said Pitt.

Dru thought so, too. She wouldn't be quite so embarrassed if nobody could know her again.

"Any rings in that chest?" Pitt asked. "Humphrey says there's gold rings go with that outfit."

"Not any more." Dru had gone through the chest thoroughly.

"He sold them, then," Pitt said to Humphrey. He lis-

79

tened, then cocked his left eye up at Dru. "Where in her nose?"

Dru was glad the rings had been stolen.

"Can't use the hatbox with that costume," Pitt told her.

There was no basket, but at the animals' urging Dru made a pouch from string and a square of her torn petticoat. It was grimy from cleaning the caravan.

"The hatbox looks better," said Dru.

"Nobody's going to see it," said Pitt. "You wear it under those drapes. Hang it under your arm, then bring the herbs out like magic."

"Like this?"

"No! Make it look important, like me going up and down to choose the right fortune or Humphrey acting too sick to dance. Make them *want*."

Dru practiced in front of the little mirror until she could produce a packet with a graceful flourish. Humphrey tapped a few steps in approval.

"It'll do," said Pitt.

They were talking when Dru fell asleep and gone when she woke. A commotion near the stream interrupted her breakfast of cheese. Before she could investigate, Pitt came hop-flopping toward her with a kicking toad in his beak. Humphrey trotted close behind. Dru grabbed the hatbox and ran to meet them, lifting the lid so Pitt could drop in the toad. Dru had worried about the snake being restless with hunger but she hadn't dared let it out to hunt.

"Thank you," she told Pitt. "And you, too, Humphrey." It had taken teamwork to catch the toad.

The snake was sluggish after eating. It hung around Dru's neck as if playing dead.

"Won't impress people like that," said Pitt.

"It will if people get close enough." Dru hoped that was true. Wearing a dead snake looked even sillier than wearing a live one.

Humphrey and Pitt escorted her as far as they dared, Humphrey walking beside her, Pitt practicing his flying.

"Try the inns," was their last bit of advice and Pitt pointed out the street where the most expensive one was.

Dru draped the scarf over her nose and set off.

❧ CHAPTER EIGHT ❧

She knew better than to use the front door even if the doorman, in a uniform fancier than anything in the chest, hadn't stared at her. She turned into a courtyard, searching for the kitchen.

Though it was mid-morning, people sat eating at cloth-covered tables under shade trees. They stared at Dru, smiling and nudging each other. A man carried a tray through a door, probably to the kitchen.

Dru started after him, then thought what Mrs. Grainger would say if someone wore a snake into her kitchen. She'd have to get rid of it if she wanted to sell any herbs. She should never have listened to Pitt! She turned to leave and bumped into a tall, angry man.

"Leave the premises at once," he whispered fiercely.

The bump had disturbed the snake. The hissed *s*'s alarmed it. It raised its head level with Dru's eyes, flattened its neck and swayed there, tongue darting. The man stepped back, his face white. The snake lowered its head and went back to dozing. Dru was standing in a patch of sun.

The tone of the whispers changed to wonder. Chairs

scraped as people rose to see better. Dru fished a packet of bergamot from her robes. The scent drifted over her.

"Herbs gathered by time and moon, spellbound to your need." Her voice came out high and cracked, first from strain, then on purpose. It seemed to fit a snake-guarded herb seller.

The prices Pitt had advised her to ask were high but people paid them without question. Dru soon realized it wasn't the herbs they wanted but a chance to stand close while paying and risk the snake hissing at them. Dru left before it got frightened enough to roll over and play dead.

Business wasn't quite as brisk at the second inn but she sold the last few packets to people who stopped her on the street. She put the snake in the empty pouch and found one of the flights of stairs that connected each street to the ones above and below. A girl in a gray dress with starched white collar and cuffs was hurrying up them. She stopped when she saw Dru.

"Please," she called, "are you the lady with the snake?"

"Sally!"

Sally leaned against the stair rail. "How did . . .?" Her face brightened. "Do you sell fortunes, too?"

Dru remembered to pull the scarf from her face.

"Dru!" Sally opened her arms. They hugged each other, babbling questions neither answered until Sally pushed Dru away and demanded to know how she'd gotten to Summerfalls.

"Willie told me you'd run away," she said.

"Willie? From the stables? What's he doing here?"

"My father sent him after me. He's even offered to give my aunt part of the money back."

"*What?*"

Sally shrugged. "Well, since we left, he has to hire people. I guess it's cheaper to give the money back."

Only if he planned to have Sally working at the inn the rest of her life. While Dru was trying to find a way to point this out, Sally said, "I wouldn't mind going back if it weren't for Willie." She turned and went down the stairs with Dru. "You were right about my aunt wanting a maid. I only get out when she takes her nap or goes visiting or to play alquerque. And look at my new wardrobe." She held out her arms. "A uniform!"

They crossed a street and went down more stairs.

"You said you wouldn't mind going back if it weren't for Willie?" Dru made it a question.

"It's that midnight spell. It's going to work, Dru." Sally stopped and turned to look at Dru. A tear ran down one cheek. "My father will make me marry Willie so he'll have both of us working for nothing. And Willie will marry me so he can get the inn. Oh, Dru, I don't want to marry Willie!"

Dru lent her the end of a veil to wipe her face. "The spell isn't working, Sally. And you don't have to go back to the inn."

She started Sally back down the stairs, telling her about the caravan. Sally interrupted to ask if Pitt still sold fortunes.

"He's retired," Dru told her and continued the story of their journey. When she finished, they'd reached the busy streets of lower Summerfalls.

Sally took Dru's money and did the bargaining. Dru draped the scarf over her face and pretended to understand nothing. She was alarmed at the prices. Though Sally wheedled and haggled them down, they were still so high that when they'd bought as much food as Dru could carry, there were only three coins left from what she'd considered a small treasure.

Sally carried half the packages back up the stairs. The street where her aunt was staying was one of the middle ones. They followed it along the mountainside past the last houses to where it vanished in a pile of boulders.

Sally glanced at the sun. "I have to go. She'll be waking soon."

"You just keep going past these boulders until you reach a stream and then follow it . . ."—Dru looked back at the hillside town and guessed—"upstream. You'll find the camp."

"Not in the dark."

And not alone, Dru could almost hear her say. Sally didn't trust the outdoors, especially at night.

"I'll meet you at the road," Sally said.

"But I don't know when we'll leave."

"I'll wait." Sally looked brave and determined.

Dru didn't tell her she might have to wait most of the night. Alone. Dru wished she could work a Heartening spell but she had no motherwort. She had no more herbs at all. And just when Sally needed her.

Sally must have been thinking along the same paths. She said, "I still have that Safe Journey spell," hugged Dru, packages and all, lifted her skirts and ran back toward the houses.

Dru watched her go out of sight, then turned and walked slowly to the stream. By the time she reached it, she'd decided that she had to tell Pitt and Humphrey she'd met Sally (they had to be warned that Willie was in Summerfalls) but perhaps she wouldn't mention that Sally was joining them. It would only upset Pitt sooner than he needed to be and she'd have to hear him complaining most of the night.

She'd guessed right. She was downstream from the camp and much closer than she'd thought. Not even the horse was in sight. They were probably waiting upstream to greet her. She set the packages inside the caravan door, took the snake from the pouch and hurried to find the animals.

Pitt found her first, swooping past her face and making her jump. Humphrey was napping against a sunwarmed rock. Dru sat beside him and told about her day. Humphrey and Pitt congratulated themselves on her success but were silent when she told about Sally. It was Willie who worried Dru.

"I don't trust him," she said. "And anybody could have seen us when we drove through lower Summerfalls."

"Or when you were down there today, spending like a Paphippany merchant," said Pitt.

"I had my face covered. And Sally would never tell anyone about us."

But Humphrey was scrambling to his feet.

"I'll go," Pitt told him and flapped off as high and fast as he could. He was soon back to report, "He's here, in the caravan."

Humphrey grunted a question about Bob.

"In the woods," Pitt told him. "He'll have to catch him first."

Willie didn't have to catch Bob at all. He could bring a horse from Summerfalls to haul the caravan away. Dru hunched over, staring at the ground between her shoes. She should never have listened to Pitt, all his talk about making people want and pretending to be some kind of a Dr. Blessing with a snake hanging around her neck. She just hoped it wasn't in the caravan with Willie. He wasn't fooled any more by its imitations.

Dru straightened, thinking hard. Then she smiled and announced, "We'll call the bailiff!"

Pitt glared at Humphrey with his right eye. "And you keep saying she's smart."

"No, wait!" Dru told him. "*We*'ll be the bailiffs. We'll make him *want* to leave."

After he'd heard her plan, Pitt said, "Chancy. Takes timing."

But it was all they could think of.

❧ CHAPTER NINE ❧

Dru crept under a bush behind the caravan. Pitt chose a branch that sagged with his weight just enough to put him the right distance above her head. Then they waited for Humphrey to guide Bob around to their left and start him charging at the camp. Dru couldn't imagine the horse going faster than a walk, but any hoofbeats would help make Willie think the bailiff and his men were coming.

While they waited, Dru chanted over a pine branch on her lap. It was just the Purifying spell she'd worked for each room of the inn last New Year's Day and the best she could do without spell book and herbs. But since everyone except her uncle and Mrs. Grainger considered Willie a pestilence, it might help.

From behind and to the left came a snort, then a questioning whinny. Dru lifted the spellbound branch over her head. Pitt stepped onto it. There was the sound of hooves on rock, then a startled whinny. Dru opened her fingers as Pitt raised his wings. He flapped away, dipping and bobbing so that Dru feared he'd hit the back of the caravan. He cleared it, dropping the pine branch on the roof. He flew more easily then, veering to a tree on Dru's right.

Now they surrounded the caravan except for the stream. They wanted Willie to run that way. It was the longest way back to Summerfalls and if he thought dogs were tracking him, he would wade. That would slow him even more, giving Dru and the animals a chance to leave.

Bob neighed and threshed in bushes to Dru's left. Humphrey's grunts sounded more like dog barks than Dru had thought possible.

She cupped her mouth and shrieked in her herb seller's voice, "There, bailiff! In there! Hurry!"

She tried a whinny but sounded less like a horse than Humphrey did a dog. She grabbed stones and threw them at the caravan to distract Willie. But he'd already left.

Pitt shouted in his bailiff's voice, "By the stream! After him!"

Hooves beat across the clearing, still at a walk but faster than Bob's usual pace. Humphrey woofed and barked somewhere near the stream. Dru circled the caravan. Only Bob was in sight, standing on the bank and staring downstream. She waited until he lowered his head to drink, then trudged up the ramp, dreading what she would see.

The packages had been kicked away from the door, but as far as she could remember, they were all there.

The cupboard and chest looked just as she'd left them. Pitt flew through the door, came to an unsteady landing and scuttled under the lower bunk. He came out and announced his coins were still there.

"We scared him away before he could steal anything," said Dru.

"No, we didn't," Pitt told her. "He had something but I couldn't see what. He was already leaving, had his back to me."

Dru sank cross-legged onto the floor. "Then we didn't scare him. It was all for nothing."

From the ramp, Humphrey snuffled something comforting, probably that the plan had been good and had worked.

"Thank you," Dru told him.

"Count everything," said Pitt.

Humphrey came in to help. Dru gathered up the packages and rechecked them as she stowed them in the cupboard. Everything she'd bought was there. She wondered if Pitt expected her to count cups and forks.

"Here," squawked Pitt. "A money-making machine."

Neither Humphrey nor Dru could see anything wrong with the stack until Pitt pointed with his beak. The end of one box was carved differently. Dru lifted off boxes to reach the odd one. The lid was inlaid with ivory.

"It's beautiful," murmured Dru. She ran her fingertips lightly over it.

"Costly," said Pitt. "What's inside?"

There was a folded game board inlaid with squares and diagonals. Felt-lined niches held playing pieces like knobbed gumdrops, half carved of light wood, half of dark.

"What kind of game is it?" said Dru.

Neither Humphrey nor Pitt knew. But they agreed Willie had left it so they wouldn't discover a machine was missing until they were far away.

"It must have taken him a while to find something the right size," said Dru. "So he couldn't have followed Sally and me today. He must have seen us drive in from the ferry."

Pitt was still suspicious. "How'd he know what to bring? How a money-machine looks?"

"I suppose we'll never know," lied Dru. She planned to ask Sally first thing. To her alarm, Pitt wanted to leave early, as if they were going to cross a ferry. "Why? Willie won't be back."

"Bailiff might, the real one, if your friend tries selling that machine in Summerfalls."

"Willie's no friend of mine," Dru told the raven. "And if we leave early, we'll be seen."

"Be seen any time of night around here," Pitt grumbled. "Best put some road behind us."

He flapped into the bushes where Humphrey had already disappeared. Dru didn't think Sally could sneak away early. And even if she could, she had a long walk to where the caravan would meet the road.

Dru changed her clothes and washed in the cold

stream. She, too, felt safer at a distance from the caravan. She took a pot upstream to pick berries until the sun dipped behind the peaks and she could no longer tell ripe from green.

When she returned to the caravan, Bob was waiting patiently between the shafts. Dru hitched him as usual but dawdled over her late supper (dried meat, fresh bread and two bowls of berries with milk) until she had to stumble to the stream and wash her bowl and spoon in the dark.

"You planning to wait for moonrise?" squawked Pitt.

He perched on the driver's seat, complaining about her slowness while she cleared the campsite. She pretended to have more trouble than she really did working in the dark. When she could delay no longer, she climbed up beside Pitt and told Humphrey to lead Bob back down to the road.

They stopped before reaching it so Dru could help Humphrey into the driver's seat and arrange his blanket and shawl. Pitt ducked through the opening to the upper bunk. Dru led Bob onto the road and took her time tucking the reins into Humphrey's blanket. She was glad a carriage driver yelled at them for blocking the road. It would alert Sally they were there if she didn't already know.

She stroked Bob's nose and murmured, "Take your time."

He snorted and flicked an ear. Dru didn't know what that meant, if anything. She climbed onto the seat beside

Humphrey and pulled down her hood, but not so far that she couldn't watch the sides of the road.

The moon rose behind them and, as Pitt had predicted, the road was busy. From overheard bits of conversation, Dru guessed people were driving out to see the falls in moonlight. She could hear the roar of water when they passed the turnoff. They met no carriages after that and Dru gave up all hope of Sally.

She took back the reins and Pitt climbed onto the seat between her and Humphrey. But Dru was too busy fighting back tears to talk.

"You can stop worrying now," Pitt told her.

Dru grunted, like Humphrey.

The road was steep and tiring and Bob stopped twice to rest, but he was moving easily over a straight, level section when he stopped again. Dru looked up, startled. A cloaked figure stood in the road, arms spread wide to stop them. Bob's ears flicked.

"Bailiff?" whispered Dru.

"Thief," guessed Pitt.

"Are you the lady with the snake?" called a shaky voice.

"*Sally!*" Dru scrambled to the ground and hugged her cousin.

"Oh, Dru, I'm so glad to see you!" Sally was almost sobbing. "I thought you'd never come or that I'd missed you. I was so frightened . . . the dark and the noises . . . ."

In his bailiff's voice, Pitt said, "What do you want?"

Sally straightened and lifted her head. "I'm going to Iskany."

"Not with us, you aren't!"

Humphrey's chuckle shook the caravan.

"Wait." Sally ran across the road and returned leading a horse. Lumpy flour sacks hung like saddlebags. "I just want to ride along. All I need is a place to sleep. The floor will do."

"Floor's taken," Pitt told her.

"There's the upper bunk," said Dru, and quickly asked where Sally had gotten the horse, though she feared she already knew. She did.

"It's my aunt's carriage horse but she won't miss it until tomorrow. Then she'll blame Willie. He's gone, too, but she doesn't know it yet." She giggled. "Maybe she'll think he carried me off."

"Tell me on the way," Dru told her. "We have to hurry."

Pitt complained loudly to Humphrey about "poor things" while Dru put Sally's flour sacks inside the caravan. One was packed with clothes. The other, Sally told her, held food. She'd prepared better than Dru had.

The horse was smaller and sleeker than Bob and wore a folded blanket instead of a saddle. Sally had to climb to the driver's seat to mount. She rode alongside, chattering from relief about her aunt who'd come to Summerfalls to find another husband and the elderly Mr. Force she'd decided on.

"She learned to play alquerque so she could see him

94

every night." Sally interrupted herself to explain that alquerque was a game much played in Iskany and brought this season to Summerfalls by royalty. "Now everybody's playing it. They have alquerque teams and alquerque evenings and alquerque clubs and a big summer tournament."

"And fancy alquerque game sets," Dru guessed.

She was right again. When Sally saw the inlaid box, she recognized it immediately as one of a set Mr. Force had had made for his alquerque evenings. Willie had attended the last one with Sally's aunt.

"Trying to make Mr. Force jealous, I guess," Sally told Dru. "I wonder what else Willie took?"

"Enough to get him downriver," said Dru. "That's all he talked about after he took your job, making his fortune in one of the kingdoms downriver."

It was a relief to know the bailiff would be going in the opposite direction after Willie. Sally also figured out how the stable boy had known about the money-making machines.

Letters to her aunt had told of a fake money-making machine sold at Kingstown Fair. A caravan with others had been stolen. The Kingstown bailiff, afraid the caravan thief would try to sell the other machines, had taken the one he had to all the wealthy people around Kingstown to show and warn them.

"My father was one of them. He wrote and told my aunt about it." Sally giggled sleepily. "He didn't tell her it was a fake, though. I think he hoped she'd buy one."

Then garbled stories had swept through Summerfalls. The fake Dr. Blessing became royalty from Sirrushany or a half-trained sorcerer, and the caravan a stolen carriage with spellbound machines piled under the seat. For a time, every boat docking at Summerfalls had been searched but nobody knew what they were looking for.

"Except Willie," finished Sally. "He must have seen the machine at the inn."

"And heard the right story about the caravan," said Dru. "Maybe he started all those rumors in Summerfalls."

"Maybe." Sally covered a yawn. "Can we go to bed now?"

"Yes. But we don't travel by day so you may sleep as long as you need to."

That changed as they moved farther up in the mountains. The road became a winding track, sometimes too squeezed between boulders for the caravan to pass. They had to travel by day and Pitt's practice flights became scouting trips to find them a way. Dru could have walked in two hours what they traveled in a good day. At least it gave her time to gather herbs, when she could find any.

Since they knew the bailiff wasn't following and Pitt saw no sign of people on his flights, they sat around a fire at night. Sally taught Dru to play alquerque but Dru wasn't good at plotting moves. Pitt, perched on the edge of the crate table, and Humphrey, sitting beside it, learned faster and better. They were soon playing a three-way tournament with Sally. Pitt kept the complicated score by moving his coins to different cracks under the bunk. While they moved the pieces from point to point on the board, Dru packaged her few herbs and embroidered the little cloth sacks with floss Sally had brought.

The higher they traveled, the colder the air and the sparser the forage for the animals. Sally's horse suffered the most but Bob also looked gaunt and he rested more often. Humphrey's ribs began to show and Dru and Sally were on half rations. Without Sally's supplies, they'd have been worse off than the animals.

Only Pitt fed well. There were plenty of bugs and a few mice, some of which he gave to Humphrey. The snake didn't eat at all; it curled in the hatbox and hibernated.

The worst stretch was a pass so high it had knee-deep snow and air so thin they were all short of breath. Then the road wound downhill and Dru had to lean on the hand brake to keep the caravan from bumping into Bob. The air grew less cold, and four days after the pass they saw a patch of new grass among the boulders.

Sally's horse bolted for it. Bob just walked faster but ignored the rocks and holes he usually avoided. The caravan jolted and lurched, tilting alarmingly. Things banged and crashed inside and Humphrey, who'd been napping on the floor, shrieked and squealed. Dru was too busy holding on to notice what was happening to Sally. She heard her cousin scream and was surprised to see her still clinging to the horse when it galloped back past the caravan, eyes rolling in fright. Then Bob stopped suddenly and Dru slid from the seat to the narrow floor. She crawled back up, brushed hair from her eyes and looked around.

Two dogs stood stiff-legged at the edge of the little meadow, their teeth bared. Bob pushed his nose toward one of them. The dog snarled. The horse looked back at Dru. She climbed down, wincing at the bruises she'd gotten. Humphrey made anxious noises inside the caravan. Dru tied the door open so he could see and she could talk to him while she maneuvered Bob and the caravan around and back to the trail they'd been following.

Pitt glided down to perch above the open door. "Village ahead."

"How far?" said Dru.

"Three, four days the way you're traveling. Your friend could get there tonight if her horse doesn't drop. If you're so worried about 'poor things,' better tell her that horse is too weak to race."

Dru explained about the dogs. Pitt had seen them herding goats in some of the small meadows but hadn't known they guarded the grass, too.

Dru leaned against the caravan, scratched behind Humphrey's ears and wondered how they could get some of the grass for the horses. Without it, they'd never reach the village, not even if Dru and Sally led them and left the caravan behind. And without the caravan, Dru didn't think Humphrey would reach the village.

"Where are the nearest goats?" Dru asked Pitt. "I'll talk to the herder."

"Aren't any herders."

Humphrey gruntled; Pitt translated. "We're in Iskany now."

"You mean the dogs are spellbound?" said Dru. They must be bound to the meadows. That meant somebody had to feed and water them.

Sally called and waved from down the trail. She'd found the young man who tended the dogs and made a trade; she'd play alquerque with him if the horses and Humphrey could graze as long as she won.

She grinned at Dru. "We must be in Iskany."

"Play slow," Pitt told her and flew along to watch.

The animals were still eating when Sally lost a game. On purpose, she insisted later to Pitt, to keep the horses from eating too much new grass and getting sick. She offered to play again the next morning but the young man refused. He was worried that he'd already lost enough of the thin grass to be in trouble.

As they traveled slowly down to the village, they found clumps of new weeds and budding leaves on the bushes along the stream. Wild animals ate them, too, and the horses and Humphrey had to forage long after dawn and before sunset. Without the one good meal in the meadow, they wouldn't have had the strength.

Five days after that meal, they reached the village. The horses were still thin and weak. Sally and Dru were on quarter rations.

They camped out of sight of the village. An excited

Sally helped Dru into her herb-seller costume. Humphrey and Pitt watched in gloomy silence.

"What's the matter?" said Dru.

Pitt answered. "We're in Iskany now, remember?"

Dru turned from the mirror. Her throat was so tight she could only whisper, "You're leaving?"

"Not yet. But you know what they say about Iskany, 'Every child a sorcerer.'"

Dru laughed in relief. "That can't be true. And besides, it's the end of winter here. Even if they know how to gather herbs, they'll be almost out of them by now."

"Food, too."

"Oh." Dru sat down on the chest. She'd hated it in Summerfalls that first day when cooks had shut doors on her. It was almost like people leaving.

"I'll go," Sally offered.

Dru would have let her but Sally didn't know which packet held what even with the designs stitched on them. Dru wished the snake weren't still hibernating.

But the snake wouldn't have made any difference. Dru knew it when she saw the carefully arranged gardens by three of the houses. Her mother had planted herbs that way, so they couldn't mix. There was enough growth for Dru to recognize most of the plants. If she'd still had the herbs she'd started with, she was sure she could have traded, even with the owners of the gardens. But the few herbs she'd gathered since Summerfalls were the same as those grown in the village.

She sighed and trudged up the first path, hoping somebody had run out of something. A woman who reminded Dru of her mother offered an egg for a packet of lovage. Sally would have gotten two but Dru was afraid to haggle.

She worried what Pitt would say about the egg. If it bothered him, he didn't show it. Unless that was the reason he offered his Iskany coins to buy food in the village. Dru handed them to Sally. Pitt squawked until she explained that Sally was better at bargaining.

Sally came back without even an egg.

"No food." Pitt sounded less pleased than he usually did when he'd been proven right.

Sally shook her head. "They won't take money. They say they can't use it. What's the matter, Dru?"

"If they can't travel to a place with shops . . . ." She turned to Pitt. "How far is it down the mountain?"

The raven didn't know. He probably couldn't soar high enough yet to see. Or maybe he could and the distance was even farther than Dru feared. No wonder nobody traveled over the mountains. Money wouldn't buy supplies and bringing packhorses meant they'd all starve faster.

Humphrey sat up and grunted. Pitt cocked an eye at him.

"What did he say?" said Sally.

Pitt turned to study her with the other eye. "Can you trade a money-making machine?"

"No!" said Dru. "That's cheating."

"Only if you tell them it makes money."

"Why else would anyone buy it?"

"To watch the wheels go around," snapped the raven. "This is Iskany! Machines are as rare as sorcerers in Zuus."

"But this one won't do anything."

Sally laughed and did a few dance steps. "A mystery machine! Maybe *you* can discover what it does. Yes, I can trade that!"

But she insisted on wearing a costume. She chose a rose brocade gown that had to be shortened and a pale green turban. She left holding one of the carved boxes in front of her like an offering. She was soon back with a sack of grain for the horses and a measure of mash for Humphrey.

"Nothing for us?" said Dru.

Sally gave her half a small cheese, two large onions and a loaf of dry bread.

"You were right," she told Pitt. "They don't have much food. The whole village traded this."

That worried Dru. But they journeyed another mile and made the happiest camp since crossing the mountain. Sally, Humphrey and Pitt had never abandoned their tournament but for the past week their games had been slow and silent. Once again they squawked and argued over the inlaid board. Dru sat cross-legged on the other side of the fire, making marks on the ground with a stick.

If the journey down the mountain took the same

amount of time as climbing the other side (and it would probably take longer), the last money-making machine would be traded before they were halfway down. Provided they found that many villages, and people were willing to trade. By then there'd be more forage for the animals. But for Sally and Dru there'd be only wild onions and maybe berries. It wouldn't be nearly enough.

She tossed the stick into the fire, waited until Humphrey won the game he was playing with Sally, then told them what she'd figured.

"And that's if everything goes just right," she finished. She hated to ask but it was the only thing she'd been able to think of. "Maybe we could give one of those shows?"

Sally straightened and clapped her hands. "Yes! Humphrey can dance and Pitt can sell fortunes and . . . ."

"And this is Iskany!" squawked Pitt. "Every village has a marvelous creature."

"Not here," said Dru.

But Sally was nodding. "Yes, Dru. Who do you think plays alquerque with that dog tender up the mountain? One of the dogs."

Humphrey wanted to know how good the dog was. Dru propped her elbows on her knees and her chin in her hands. Sally had set up the board and was watching Pitt play Humphrey, a sight people in any other kingdom would pay well to see. The raven was in constant motion, sidestepping along the edge of the crate, cock-ing his head this way, then that, resettling his wings. Humphrey sat like a stone until ready to move. Then he tilted his whole body forward, snapped his lips over a knobby top, jerked this way or that to place it, then tilted back. Forward, snap, move, tilt back, almost like a machine.

Dru wished they had such a machine. People in Iskany would line up to play alquerque with it even if it played no better than that dog Sally had told Pitt and Humphrey about. It was the machine that counted, like those useless money-making machines.

Dru yelled and leaped to her feet. She lifted her skirts and, while the others stared, jigged around the fire yelling, "I got it! I got it! I got it!"

❧ CHAPTER TEN ❧

"A Humphrey machine?" said Sally.

"No, just something to put around Humphrey to make him look more like a machine." Dru turned to the pig. "Excuse me, Humphrey, but you do look like one when you play alquerque."

She played part of a game with him so Pitt and Sally could watch from across the fire. They agreed.

"Even close up," Sally marveled. "You can't even see him breathe."

"Wrong color," said Pitt.

"I can make a dye to fix that," Dru told him. "It's the building I'm worried about."

But Sally had helped make repairs around the inn and all they needed to do was knock things apart and put them together in a different way.

Dru knocked slats off crates, straightened nails and carefully pried apart money-making machines, all but one which they saved to trade for food at another village. Sally did the building, but Dru figured out how Pitt could turn the cogs and wheels of two money-making machines with one handle. While Dru and Sally worked on the "machine," Humphrey and Pitt played game after game of alquerque.

Pitt made his report. "First move has less chance of winning but that won't matter unless Humphrey plays somebody as good as me. Then it's usually a draw."

"Then we'll give refunds only for wins," said Dru.

"And make them move first."

Dru shook her head. "We'll toss a coin."

Pitt made a scornful noise but Humphrey agreed with Dru. It was an Iskany game. The people would probably know the odds, too.

They set up the small platform behind the caravan and tested the "machine." Sally pushed it slowly through the rear door. It was just a large box hinged so the top half could be tilted back to show Humphrey seated within. There'd only been enough carved pieces to cover the part of the box that stuck out on the platform. Dru had lined the top half with the velvet robe she'd been using for a towel. From where she stood in front of the platform, it hardly looked crumpled and Humphrey's upper body covered the stains. Sally opened the doors in the front of the bottom half, revealing the innards of two money-making machines. She signaled Pitt and the wheels and gears began to clatter and turn.

Sally hopped down the portable steps she'd built and came to stand beside Dru. "How does it look?"

"Like a pig in a box." Dru's eyes filled with tears.

"It's daylight." Sally put an arm around her. "But it's a good thing we didn't have any more carved pieces. This way, Humphrey has to sit farther back than we planned, almost inside the door. And with that dark velvet and torchlight"—she squeezed Dru's shoulders—"he'll look just like a machine."

"I hope so." Dru wondered what happened to people in Iskany who faked machines and then charged people to play with them. It worried her enough to make Sally promise never to call Humphrey a machine, not right out. It took them a whole afternoon to agree on what to paint on a small wooden sign:

CAN YOU BEAT THE CALCULATING PIG?
SEE THE MACHINE!
PLAY ALQUERQUE WITH THE PIG—
10¢ IN CASH OR KIND—
RETURNED IF YOU WIN

Sally carried it into the next village at noon, wearing the brocade gown and the turban. Her horse glittered with gold trimmings they'd taken from the costumes and fastened to harness and saddle blanket and braided in mane and tail. Following Pitt's instructions, Sally rode slowly clear through the village and back again, loudly announcing their arrival at dusk. Then she left the sign leaning against the wall of the smithy. It was the largest village they'd found since Summerfalls.

Sally and Dru spent the afternoon rehearsing. Rather, Dru rehearsed. Sally said something different each time and always sounded natural and right. Before they took down the platform, Dru brewed a strong tea of yellow dock root, mixed it with water and washed the floor of the platform while chanting for plenty of customers.

She changed to her herb-seller costume before driving into the village. The veils were a nuisance for her when they set up the platform, careful to get the planks Humphrey used to reach the driver's seat smooth side up. They had an audience of children and old people. Humphrey and Pitt stayed hidden inside. Sally and Dru hung red curtains over the rear door and set torches where they wouldn't give too much light. Then they went back through the curtains and there was nothing to do but wait.

Dru crouched on a corner of the chest whispering her opening remarks over and over. She wished Sally could be up on the platform but Sally was needed to coax people into trading for a game.

Humphrey's snout touched her arm. Dru didn't need Pitt to tell her what he grunted.

"Thank you," she murmured and scratched behind his ears. "You'll be marvelous, too."

Then it was time. Dru draped the scarf over her face, stepped onto the platform and made as much ceremony as she could out of lighting the torches. Make it slow, make them notice, Pitt had told her.

"There's nobody out there!" she whispered when she was back inside.

"They're eating," said Pitt. "The torches will bring them back."

He was right. Each time she peeked through the curtains, more faces stared up. When she stepped onto the platform, there were more people than could possibly live in the village, all staring up at her. Her heart pounded and her throat tightened so she'd never get a word out even if she could remember one. Then her stomach began to rumble.

Her only thought was to cover the noise before somebody laughed. When her panic eased, she found herself halfway through the greeting she'd rehearsed.

"And now for the wonder of the age," she proclaimed. "Brought at terrible cost over the mountains! Seen for the very first time in Iskany! HUMPHREY THE MAGNIFICENT CALCULATING PIG!"

The curtain looped back and the box was pushed onto the platform. Sally had been watching carefully and it stopped at the edge of the paneling. The crowd murmured and pushed forward.

Sally had made rollers from parts of a money-making machine but they wouldn't support Humphrey's weight while moving. He had to climb into the box after it was in place. To cover any noise and jiggling, Dru paced back and forth, bragging about the machinery, then opening the doors to point her wand at various gears and wheels while pretending to explain how they worked. She was sweating and running out of words when Sally came around the caravan, set the portable steps in front of the platform and climbed up.

"And now," announced Dru, *"the alquerque champion of Zuus!"*

With Sally on the other side of the box, they tipped

the top half back until it rested on supports inside the caravan. There was a second of silence that sent Dru's heart dropping, then the villagers roared and clapped and shouted. Dru didn't blame them. Humphrey sat behind the alquerque board. Painted black with bark dye, he looked like royal treasure against the velvet. Though she was closer than she'd let any player stand, Dru saw no movement to show the pig was alive.

Pitt had advised her to give a demonstration. Dru chose a wide-eyed child to play one free game with Humphrey. Humphrey won the first move. Tilt, grab the knobbed piece, move it, tilt back. The crowd ohed and ahed, torn between watching Humphrey and the gears that rattled and turned below. Dru imagined poor Pitt sidestepping from one handle to the other, trying to keep up with her tapped signals.

The game was over faster than they'd planned, but Sally had been moving through the small crowd, changing the awed murmurs to the banter and laughter Dru had heard so often from the dining room at the inn. Though she persuaded only two people to play, one played three games. Humphrey lost once and Dru was happy to return the goat cheese.

When the last game ended, Sally climbed onto the platform to help Dru shut the doors over the gears and pull the box top down over Humphrey. Only they saw the deep breath he took.

Sally made the closing speech. Dru didn't listen. There was a lot of laughter and she was straining to hear Pitt's signal that Humphrey had backed safely out of the box. It came. Dru caught Sally's eye. Sally finished whatever she was saying, bowed and waved a thank you for the applause and then helped Dru push the box back through the curtains.

Like the false Dr. Blessing, they packed and left in the dark, Sally chattering about the people as if she'd been to a party.

The shows were exhausting for everyone except Sally. They gave one only when they needed food, which was less often as they moved down into kinder country.

They camped among trees again, in grassy clearings. The snake came out of hibernation. If it was confused at having wakened twice this year, it gave no sign. In a few days it had fattened enough to shed its skin. Humphrey's skin filled, too, and even Bob began to look sleek.

Dru found watercress and berries and herbs she'd seen only on old Munk's charts. It was the Iskany of the envious stories, where sorcerers kept summer all year. And Dru wished they were back in goat country.

Pitt could soar great distances now. From his long, excited conferences with Humphrey, she guessed he was searching for the refuge Humphrey remembered. She'd known they were going to leave; that was part of the bargain. But she hadn't thought it would be so soon or that they'd be so happy about it.

She might not have minded so much if Sally hadn't started looking for royalty among the young men who watched their shows. And during the dark of the moon, she searched the wide stream they camped by for a rock to use for the True Love spell. She chose one a long wade from shore.

"Those peaks look awfully uncomfortable," Dru told her.

"I know, but it's the only one we can be sure was never flooded."

"We need a willow tree."

But Sally had found that, too. With a sigh, Dru went to find a stone with a sharp cutting edge. There was a chant for washing the stone in the stream, another for cutting the willow wand (a perfect one of new growth) and still a third for burying the stone beneath the tree. Sally held the spell book so Dru could read them. She didn't need the book for the spell itself. That was easy except for wading out to the rock and standing in cold water to work it.

Dru chanted as she tied the willow wand in a knot, left over right, right over left. *This knot I tie, this knot I knit, for Sally's true love whom she has not yet met.*

Then she tossed the willow knot onto the rock and boosted Sally up after it. She waited for a moment, hoping Sally would change her mind, then waded carefully back to the bank. It was dark before she reached it. She climbed out, found a comfortable seat on the bank and dried her legs.

She felt terrible. Humphrey and Pitt were leaving soon and, if the spell worked, so was Sally. For the first time, Dru was glad her spells didn't work right. But she had no way of knowing which way this one would work wrong. And maybe in Iskany they'd all work perfectly.

She got up and walked carefully to the caravan, lit a candle stub and took out her spell book. There was spikenard, both blossom stalks and leaves, among the herbs hanging from the ceiling. Dru picked three leaves and made a tea. While it was brewing she tore a blank page from the back of her spell book, found a pencil stub in the cupboard drawer and drew a picture of Sally.

"*Hethera pethera dather and drove.*" She sprinkled the spikenard tea on the picture as she chanted. "*Ever return o'er mountain and cove.*"

She hung the picture upside down and face to the wall behind the mirror where no one would see it. Now Sally was spellbound to remain with the caravan. In case she noticed the candle's light and wondered what Dru was doing in the caravan, Dru tugged quilts from the bunks and carried them to the bank.

Humphrey lay near the fire. Pitt stood in the curve of his neck. Dru could hear them talking softly as she settled on one of the quilts. Sally's scream made them all jump.

Dru slid down the bank. There was a large splash out in the stream. Dru guessed it was Sally and waded in that direction. They met sooner than she'd expected and had to grab each other to keep from falling. Sally was sobbing about spells and Willie at the window.

"You couldn't have seen Willie," Dru told her.

"Not Willie. A monster!" Even when they were dried and wrapped in quilts by the fire, Sally insisted she'd seen a monster. "Worse than that time we saw Willie. This was big and bulgy and . . . *horrible*. Oh, Dru, I'm going to marry a monster!"

"No, you aren't. This spell was only for meeting your true love."

She'd meant it for comfort but Sally burst into tears. Humphrey made anxious noises. Even the horses were upset and restless. Bob didn't settle down for days, twitching his ears and rolling his eyes. But maybe he knew Humphrey and Pitt were leaving just as soon as they reached a place where Dru could sell her herbs. They were traveling far out of their way in case they were needed for another show.

Three days after Sally had seen the monster, they came to the end of the wild country, a ridge overlooking fields and orchards and real roads that met in a large town.

Pitt swooped down to sit on the seat beside Dru. "You can sell herbs there?"

Dru nodded, not trusting herself to speak. This was good-by. She'd seen no high-country herbs for weeks. She'd have no trouble selling them here.

She let Humphrey out of the caravan and scratched behind his ears for the last time. She could just make out his shape through her tears.

"Stop blubbering," Pitt told her. "You still got the poor snake and poor Bob and poor Sally."

"But no Pitt and Humphrey."

"Not if one of those farmers down there sees us."

Humphrey snortled softly and nudged her. Dru patted him, then wiped her eyes to watch them vanish in the bushes, Humphrey carrying the little sack she'd made for Pitt's coins, Pitt walking alongside instead of flying. Dru leaned against the caravan, remembering, until Sally cleared her throat, backed and turned her horse.

"Come on, Dru!" she urged. "The road to Farewell is down there!"

It wasn't, but they found one that led them to the Farewell road. By then Bob was behaving normally and Dru, who'd begun to wonder if they were being followed, decided the horse had just been missing Humphrey and Pitt and listening for them.

Farewell was much larger than Kingstown but the first person they asked directed them to the spell school. From there it was easy to find the shop. Munk, Jr. looked almost as old as his father. He welcomed Sally and Dru and Dru's herbs.

"My father's found no one to replace you and your mother," he told her. "My youngest son is collecting in the mountains but I don't expect much. He doesn't cure them properly, just leaves them crammed in a sack. I must bury most of what he brings."

The bell jangled as the door opened for a customer, then again for a young man who pointed a finger at Sally and Dru and shouted, "There they are! Ask them, Father, ask them what they did to Dr. Blessing!"

The complete story had to wait until the shop closed. Sally waited on customers when she could and amused the others until Munk, Jr. could discuss their needs. The young man, Jock, helped Dru prepare what he and his father declared was the best meal ever cooked in the kitchen. It was certainly the best Sally and Dru had eaten in a while. They finished the tale of their journey while the men washed and dried dishes. Dru felt like royalty, watching them.

Jock sheepishly confessed it was he who'd frightened Sally. "There's a hole near that rock. I was carrying the herb sacks and my clothes on my head."

"I thought you were a monster," said Sally.

Dru looked from one to the other and was glad of Sally's spellbound picture in the caravan.

"I was going to apologize," Jock went on, "but when you screamed so close, I fell down and my clothes got soaked."

"Not to mention the herbs," muttered his father. "Why didn't you wait until morning to cross?"

Jock flushed. "I saw their fire."

And me walking around it, thought Dru, and wanted company. Munk, Jr. nodded as if he'd thought it, too.

"I had to wait for my clothes to dry," Jock said. "By then I'd seen the lettering on the caravan and was suspicious. Father had told me about Dr. Blessing and there you were with his pig and his caravan but no Dr. Blessing or crow. I followed you to make sure."

"Until we reached the Farewell road," said Dru.

Jock looked surprised. "Yes. Then I came ahead and waited for you outside town."

He offered to atone by escorting them around Farewell. Sally accepted but Dru declined. She wanted to talk with Munk, Jr.

He didn't laugh when she said she wanted to enter the spell school. He nodded gravely, thought a moment and said, "Did you attend school in Kingstown?"

"Of course!" What sort of kingdom did he think Zuus was?

"How long?"

"Until I could read and do sums. It's the same for everyone." Then she realized what he meant. She grinned. "Two winters. I don't like sitting indoors so I learned extra fast."

"But no matter how fast you learn, it will take you more years than you've lived to learn to be a sorcerer. You must learn to make everything you use."

Dru thought of the spell she'd worked for Sally with the stone and willow wand and the washing and burying with a chant for each. But Munk, Jr. meant more than that.

"You must learn mining and smelting and the working of metals, the working and firing of clay, scutching flax, spinning and weaving it, how to grind paints and mix dyes and more."

"But I just want to know how to make my spells work right!" She explained her problem.

Munk, Jr. smiled. "Your spells aren't working wrong, Dru. They're just working."

"But . . . ."

"When one of your herbs sprouts, it takes the easiest way, the way that disturbs surrounding roots and plants the least. Spells work that way. Your spell might have closed the inn by plague or fire or your uncle's death but flood caused the least disturbance."

Dru frowned. "There must be some way to control it or you wouldn't have such good weather."

Now the man frowned. "I don't understand."

"Your sorcerers keep summer in Iskany."

Munk, Jr. laughed. "No, Dru, the good weather keeps our sorcerers here. There aren't enough of them to change the kingdom's weather even without working the control."

Dru sat up, excited. "Then there is a way to control spells!"

"Yes. It's been described to me as fencing a spell with many others so it can work only in one direction. But the control spells must also be controlled. Teaching how is the purpose of the schools."

"And it takes forever." Dru slumped in her chair.

"I can arrange an appointment." He raised a hand. "Don't decide now. I suggest you rest a few days and remove the lettering from your caravan. Jock can find some paint somewhere."

They drank chocolate and talked of old Munk and herbs and Dru's mother. Then Dru borrowed a candle and went to bed in the caravan. She heard Sally outside, whispering and giggling with Jock, long before she came inside. First thing next morning, Dru checked the picture behind the mirror. It was still there.

Jock collected two dozen paint pots, none full and each with a different color. He eyed them doubtfully. "There'll be enough if we mix them together."

"What color would we get?" said Dru.

"Brown . . . gray . . . something muddy."

That was a terrible thing to do to such clear, bright colors. "Can't we use them like this?"

They did, covering the caravan with swirling leaves and blossoms and stems of red and yellow and purple and bright blue, each bordered with two or three bands of contrasting colors. Dru painted the spaces between with light blue, the color of the sky behind the mountains. Jock used the last bits of paint on complicated borders around sides, front and back.

They gathered almost as many watchers as some of Humphrey's alquerque games. Most were customers from the shop. Dru inspected them with quick glances, trying to pick out the spell-school students. Jock confirmed her guesses. The students were the pale, thin ones with lines of strain around their mouths and eyes. Even the young ones had them. But it was the indoor look that decided Dru. It reminded her of Mrs. Grainger and the inn.

While Dru and Jock painted, Sally helped in the shop, cleaned the living quarters behind it and shopped in the square each morning. Dru went with her once. Sally seemed to know half the people in Farewell. But she spent all her free time with Jock. She even joined his alquerque club.

The True Love spell had worked. And, as usual, Dru

had been the one disturbed. It wasn't fair. She hadn't even wanted to work the spell. But she didn't need to worry. She had the spellbound picture behind the mirror. All the same, she fretted over having chosen to paint the caravan in a way that took so many days.

At last it was done.

Sally clapped her hands and proclaimed it beautiful. "But it has no lettering. Nobody will know who you are."

"I doubt that," said Munk, Jr.

Dru turned to look at him but he hadn't been making a joke. He pointed to various parts of the designs.

"There's tansy and pennyroyal, marshmallow and yarrow. You've painted them bright and twisted in a pattern but anyone in Iskany will know what you sell."

"But that isn't why I painted them." She'd painted what she knew and loved, hardly realizing what she was doing. She remembered now. Jock or his father had told her. Herbalists were given safe passage in Iskany. She could go anywhere she pleased.

And Sally would go with her; she had to. But the feeling that gave her wasn't happiness. It was satisfaction flavored with something darker. Maybe that spell was working out through her, too.

Munk, Jr. interrupted her thoughts. "I assume you do not wish to attend spell school."

Dru shook her head. "I'd just learn to make bigger disturbances."

Everybody laughed except Sally. In the caravan, after

supper, she asked Dru, "What are you going to do?" She was combing her hair in front of the mirror, which made Dru uneasy.

"We'll go somewhere." Dru flung out her arms. "Anywhere! That's what you said at the inn. Remember?"

Sally nodded and smiled. "And we did."

"But we haven't gone *everywhere*. I'll make a list of supplies and we can leave as soon as the paint dries."

Sally looked so . . . so . . . Dru didn't know what until Jock stuck his head in the caravan door and urged Sally to hurry or they'd miss the first round of the alquerque tournament. Then Dru remembered. It was the look Sally had had when Dru met her on the steps in Summerfalls. She flopped back on the bunk and lay a long time thinking.

She got up and took the picture from behind the mirror, unbound and destroyed it. Then she lay down and cried, which didn't make sense because she was feeling better. The dark, guilty feeling was gone.

She helped Jock prepare breakfast but waited until they were all seated to tell them what she'd decided.

"I'm going back to the mountains and collect herbs."

"Good!" said Munk, Jr. "I'll tell you about the rare ones and lend you supplies if you give me first choice."

"How long will we be gone?" Sally couldn't keep the sorrow from her voice.

Jock looked bereft. Dru passed him the crock of honey.

"I'm going alone," she told them. "That caravan's too small for two."

Sally gave her a long look.

"We'll expect you to winter here," Munk, Jr. said. "We have drying facilities in the attic."

"You must come back in time for the wedding," said Jock.

His father was the only one surprised and then only, he claimed, by his son's sudden good sense.

"You must work us a spell for happiness," said Sally.

"There isn't one," Dru told her. At least her spell book had none and she was glad. She wouldn't be able to bear the disturbance it would cause.

She didn't leave for three hectic days. Munk, Jr. provisioned the caravan as if it were a fortress preparing for siege. Jock drew her maps. Sally washed and mended her clothes.

"I'll make new ones before you come back," she promised. She also insisted Dru take the spare horse. Jock agreed.

"You can't reach the best herbs with the caravan," he told her.

She left at first light. Sally cried. Dru cried that night. She'd never been so lonely, not even the night Sally had left the inn. She didn't even have the snake to worry about.

It had found carrion plants in the far corner of Munk, Jr.'s garden. The bad-smelling flowers attracted flies which brought more toads than the snake would ever eat. The hognose spent its days between the plants and a sunny stretch of brick path.

Dru sighed and wiped her eyes. She lit a candle, found pencil and paper but didn't draw or work the spell. It wasn't fair to make Humphrey and Pitt unhappy just because she was.

She couldn't help watching the birds, though the road she took was different and all soaring birds looked black.

Late the third day, Bob pricked his ears and stepped out faster than Dru had known he could. The horse tied to the caravan whinnied, but in joy, it seemed, instead of protest. Bob topped a rise and stopped.

Under a bush sat a pig. Beside him stood a raven, peering up at Dru with his left eye.